"Step forward. It's time to widen your world."

Annalise guided Juan's hand to move the stick a bit more in front of him and beyond his feet. "That should be the farthest you swing the cane to the side. Otherwise, you'll be contacting things that aren't in your path."

"Evie showed me, but I'm having a tough time judging how far to go."

"Relax, Juan, and let your muscles do the work. *They* know what to do."

"Easier said than done," he grumbled.

"Relax."

"How can I do that when you're touching me?"

Abruptly she was aware how close they stood. She'd been focused on helping him, but couldn't ignore his fresh masculine scent and the warmth of the skin along his hand. She knew she should step away. She wasn't in any hurry to get remarried.

Remarried? Where had *that* thought come from? She needed to shake it out of her head.

She'd already made a big mistake when she'd fallen in love with Boaz. He'd left her with a broken heart and shattered dreams long before he'd died. She wouldn't risk that again...

Jo Ann Brown loves stories with happily-ever-after endings. A former military officer, she is thrilled to write about finding that forever love all over again with her characters. She and her husband (her real hero who knows how to fix computer problems quickly when she's on deadline) divide their time between Western Massachusetts and Amish country in Pennsylvania. She loves hearing from readers, so drop her a note at joannbrownbooks.com.

Books by Jo Ann Brown

Love Inspired

Amish of Prince Edward Island

Building Her Amish Dream
Snowbound Amish Christmas
Caring for Her Amish Neighbor

Green Mountain Blessings

An Amish Christmas Promise
An Amish Easter Wish
An Amish Mother's Secret Past
An Amish Holiday Family

Amish Spinster Club

The Amish Suitor
The Amish Christmas Cowboy
The Amish Bachelor's Baby
The Amish Widower's Twins

Visit the Author Profile page at LoveInspired.com for more titles.

Caring for Her Amish Neighbor

Jo Ann Brown

LOVE INSPIRED
INSPIRATIONAL ROMANCE

LOVE INSPIRED®

INSPIRATIONAL ROMANCE

Recycling programs
for this product may
not exist in your area.

ISBN-13: 978-1-335-59684-0

Caring for Her Amish Neighbor

For questions and comments about the quality of this book, please contact us
at CustomerService@Harlequin.com.

Love Inspired
22 Adelaide St. West, 41st Floor
Toronto, Ontario M5H 4E3, Canada
www.LoveInspired.com

Printed in U.S.A.

Jesus cried and said, He that believeth on me,
believeth not on me,
but on him that sent me. And he that seeth me
seeth him that sent me.
I am come a light into the world,
that whosoever believeth on me
should not abide in darkness.
—*John* 12:44–46

For Uncle Maurice,
who showed me that being blind
didn't mean he couldn't see with his loving heart.
I miss you.

Chapter One

Prince Edward Island, Canada

The goats were restless.

Juan Kuepfer frowned as he stepped out of his farmhouse. He had a *gut* view of the red sand beaches flanking the Brudenell River. He looked across the yard to the barn where he'd finished milking his cows a few hours ago. He'd been up before the sun. It had chased away last night's rain clouds so he could enjoy the brilliantly blue spring sky. After more than a year in Prince Edward Island, he was, at long last, living in his own house on his own land. He'd stayed with his brother, Lucas, while they stole time from other tasks on their farms and for their family and neighbors, to fix Juan's house.

Juan had been patient, which hadn't been easy. He'd waited so long for the day when he could step out the door and be close to his barn. It was as he'd dreamed it would be through two long and difficult Prince Edward Island winters.

He heard the goats bleat again. The horses stirred, and the geese and chickens were on edge. The sheep acted oblivious to whatever was upsetting the other livestock, but he knew what it was.

"That ridiculous dog," he said through clenched teeth.

It belonged to his neighbor. A black pug that had no more brains than the sheep and loved to chase his animals after sneaking across the field between his farm and his neighbor's place. Each time the annoying dog came, it reminded him of the loss of his friend Boaz Overgard, and how everything might have been different if Juan had been with Boaz the day he died.

Boaz was gone, leaving behind a widow, a handicapped *kind* and his *grossmammi* Fern...and a willful, witless dog.

The goats bleated frantically. Running onto the porch, he grabbed a spade and dashed toward his barn. On its far side was the field where the first sprigs of green emerged from the bright rust-red soil. Waving the spade should scare the critter away. If not, he'd slap it against the ground to send the black dog scurrying home.

As he came around the barn, a sharp squeal bombarded his ears. So loud he halted in midstep as if he'd slammed into the barn's wall. He dropped the spade and clamped his hands over his ears. Ahead of him, his horses reared in terror, but he couldn't hear their whinnying. He'd been deafened by the screech. They raced toward the far side of their paddock. The cows and goats fled, too. Sharp feathers hit his arm as the chickens and geese half flew, half ran past him. The sheep backed away.

What was happening? What—?

A blast of sound hit him like a giant fist in the center of his chest. He was lifted off his feet. Knocked backward. Something boiling struck him, searing his skin and sending agony along his arms and face. Then he hit the ground. Pain exploded in his head.

Then nothing.

Where was he?

Where was he?

Where was he?

The question repeated in his mind as he began to crawl through a dark pit lined with pain. Every bit of him hurt. Really hurt.

Who was he? He searched his paralyzed brain. He had a name. He'd heard it every day of his life. He could almost say it, but what was it?

"He's moving," someone said. A woman. Who?

The surface beneath him shifted as a deeper voice asked, "Can you hear me, Juan?"

Juan. His name was Juan. If he had an ounce of energy, he'd twirl around in delight like a *kind*. His name was Juan.

But he didn't move. Even thinking of doing so elicited a pulse of dizziness.

"Juan, can you hear me? It's me. Your brother Lucas."

Lucas? He recognized that name, too, and his brother's familiar face flashed through his mind. Lucas had inherited his dark hair and flashing brown eyes from their *grossmammi*, who'd been born and raised in Mexico. "Tall, dark and handsome" described Lucas while Juan was shorter with light brown hair and mundane blue eyes. He didn't make women's heads turn as his brother did.

"Can you hear me, Juan?" His brother's voice was becoming frantic.

Juan pushed aside his vague thoughts. *"Ja."* He

didn't open his eyes, because the slightest motion sent agony thundering through his skull. "Wh-wh-what happened?"

"We aren't sure."

"We?" Belatedly, he recalled he'd heard a woman speak. He'd thought it'd been his imagination.

He *was* in his room in his house. He was lying in his bed beneath the familiar quilt *Mamm* had made for him before he left Ontario. What was a woman doing there?

As if he'd asked aloud, his brother said, "Annalise found you. She's been waiting with me for the *doktor* to arrive."

Annalise? Annalise Overgard? Her face was clear in his mind, too. Recently—when?—she'd chased *Grossmammi* Fern's little dog onto his land. When he'd asked her to keep the dog at home, his gaze had collided with wide dark brown eyes. The breeze had gently teased wisps of blond hair along high cheekbones on either side of her upturned nose. Her delicate features hadn't matched the strong emotions in her eyes. Though she was more than ten inches shorter than his nearly six feet, the stern set of her slender shoulders beneath her black apron and dress of the same color had warned she wasn't someone to mess with.

Annalise Overgard, the widow of his late friend, was the one person he couldn't face because of his guilt of not being with Boaz on the day of his death. He groaned, not sure if from the painful memories or his throbbing pulse.

"Doktor?" He started to open his eyes, but his lashes brushed against something over them. What was going on?

"Don't," Annalise said, grasping his wrists to keep his hands away from his eyes. "Leave the washcloth in place until the *doktor* gets here. It's keeping the ointment on your face."

"Ointment?" A stinging wave crossed his cheeks and the side of his jaw. His fingers found goo on his skin. He held them to his nose.

Petroleum jelly. Why had someone lathered his face with stinky goo?

"You were burned," Lucas said in the same near whisper Annalise used. "In an explosion. In the barnyard."

Juan stiffened, ignoring the earthquake of agony clamping around every muscle. "What about—?"

"Your animals are fine," Annalise replied. "It took us a few minutes to find the chickens. They were roosting in the trees."

Relief filled him, but his shock was stronger. He hadn't expected Annalise to discern what was worrying him. Boaz had complained about how obtuse she was when she'd refused to understand why he wanted to go lobstering instead of working on his farm. She couldn't have guessed her husband would die when he fell off a boat while out on the ocean, but she also hadn't understood how Boaz needed time away from work—and from her.

Another bolt of astonishment hit Juan. How could he remember so much about her when he hadn't been able to recall his own name? So many questions… He was about to ask another when a wave of nausea rolled over him. He gripped the mattress to keep from being washed away.

Footfalls came from the direction of his bedroom door. Who was it?

"I'm Dr. Armstrong," said a man with a deep voice. "Tell me about your head."

"It aches."

The *doktor* murmured something, then asked, "Do you feel dizzy when you move?"

"Ja."

"Sick to your stomach?"

"Ja."

Another pause, then the *doktor* asked, "Do you know your name?"

As proud as if he'd won best of show with one of his cows, he said, *"Ja.* It's Juan."

"Juan what?"

"Juan…" What was the rest of his name? He searched his aching mind, but everywhere he looked, the doors to his memories were closed. Then one opened. "Kuepfer. My name is Juan Kuepfer."

Fingers rested on his left arm and gave it a gentle squeeze. Annalise? She was offering him comfort? He hadn't expected that after the harsh words he'd thrown at her…when?

Had the confrontation about her dog been yesterday or last week? It was as if time had curled like a worm, contorting in every possible direction as it overlapped and went nowhere.

Odd how he could remember the name of his friend's widow but had trouble recalling his own.

Dr. Armstrong continued his examination and his questions. Juan tried to respond to each. For most, he knew the answer. A few he wasn't sure about, like the calendar date and which province they were in. Then he recalled it was Prince Edward Island.

Other questions he couldn't answer, though he believed he should have been able to. What was wrong with his brain?

"Juan," the *doktor* said, "your memory lapses and

physical symptoms are consistent with a concussion. I'd like to check your balance and then do a quick vision test. Do you think you can sit?"

"Of course I can." When he put his hands against the mattress, the nausea returned, and he had to clamp his lips not to vomit.

"Relax," Dr. Armstrong urged. "I'll check your balance later."

Juan reached for the cloth on his face, eager to have the exam finished so he could lie still and keep his stomach from doing jumping jacks. Gentle hands halted him. They were small, so they had to be Annalise's.

Dismay taunted him as he thought of his stumbling words and uncertain answers. Why did she have to witness this?

The cloth was removed, but a hand hovered above his eyes. "Open your eyes, Juan. I know the light may hurt at first, though we've got the shades down."

He opened his eyes. Didn't he? Was the *doktor*'s hand over his eyes? Darkness surrounded him. He groped for the man's hand. It wasn't there. He blinked. Once, twice, then a third time. The blackness didn't shift.

Air wafted in front of his face as Dr. Armstrong asked, "How many fingers do you see?"

"I can't see anything!"

Annalise pressed her hand over her mouth as she stared at her neighbor's horrified face. Juan couldn't see? Had his eyes been burned like his cheeks and forehead? The image of him on the ground, surrounded by small fires as if a bomb had gone off, burst into her mind.

Everything in the destruction area had been wet, and puddles had claimed spots where the earth had been torn away. Debris of all sorts and sizes had been scattered everywhere. Chunks of metal bigger than she was sat atop others.

A charred chassis had tilted on two wheels. The twisted lump of steel had been so contorted she couldn't guess what it had been before the explosion. A dark spot halfway across the field might have been a wheel.

Acrid smoke had made her sinuses feel as if someone had scraped them with a sharp knife. A slimy mist had clung to her. She'd coughed and waved her hand, but shooing away the smoke had been useless as more swirled around her. Should she have hurried away?

She couldn't. Not until she'd been certain the only damage was to whatever had blown up.

It hadn't been. Annalise looked at the bed. Lucas's face had drained of color. Dr. Armstrong's hands shook as he reached for his bag. He pulled out a handheld device.

"I'm going to use this ophthalmoscope to look deep into Juan's eyes," the *doktor* said.

Silence filled the room except for the ticking of an alarm clock on the nightstand. She wondered if the Kuepfer brothers were holding their breaths, too, while the *doktor* had Juan look up and down, then left and right. She released her breath when the *doktor* stepped away from the bed. He put two cotton pads covered with ointment over Juan's eyes, holding them in place with gauze wrapped around his head.

"What's wrong?" Juan asked. "Why can't I see?"

"I'm covering your eyes to prevent you from straining them," the *doktor* said as he finished securing the gauze. "I can't see any damage, but vision can be affected by a concussion. Most injured people regain most of their eyesight within a few hours."

"What about the others? How can I farm if I can't see?"

Dr. Armstrong patted Juan on the shoulder. "Don't search for trouble where there might not be any."

"I can't look for anything!" Frustration sliced through his words.

"A concussion takes time to heal."

"How long?"

"You've got approximately six weeks before we'll know if your vision will return. If there's no improvement by then…" He cleared his throat. "Well, let's take it one step at a time. I'll schedule preliminary tests for you at the hospital in Montague. If necessary, we can have additional testing done in Charlottetown later. The best thing now is rest."

The *doktor* motioned toward the door, his eyes shifting from Lucas to Annalise. She was shocked. Why would she be part of a conversation about Juan?

"I'll be back tomorrow to check on you, Juan," Dr. Armstrong said before picking up his bag.

Lucas swayed as he came around the bed, and Annalise linked their arms so he didn't fall. She guessed his knees were shaking as hard as his hands. Were his thoughts like hers when she'd learned her daughter, Evie, was blind? The helpless anger, the pointless questions of wondering why it had to happen to her family, the negotiating with God to make it possible for her daughter to see. She'd come to understand they must accept God's challenges along with His grace, but it'd taken more than a year for her to reach that point. Boaz never had.

Pushing the thought aside, she wondered how long it would take Lucas to accept what had happened. More important, how long would it take Juan? She prayed God would grant him healing.

Dr. Armstrong closed the door and walked along the hall without speaking. When they stood in the kitchen with its maple cabinets and new wood floor, too far from Juan's room for him to hear, he said, "You need to know that if his eyesight doesn't return within six weeks, there's a good chance it won't."

Lucas sucked in his breath. "Never?"

"Let's not go there before we have to," the *doktor* said. "I'm sure you've got questions."

She did, but she was a far-from-welcome outsider in this house. "Lucas, I'll leave you to discuss this with the *doktor*."

"*Danki* for coming, Annalise." He hesitated, then said, "It was kind of you under the circumstances."

She nodded, not sure what she could say. Assuring him she'd make sure Juan had food the rest of the week and that she'd share their need for help on the farm, she went to the door.

"Have his eyes been burned?" Lucas asked as she opened it.

The *doktor* replied, "No, but his whole brain is in shock. The good news is brains know how to heal themselves."

Closing the door, Annalise took a single step, then dropped to a bench on the porch. Boaz had told her how the brothers along with two of their cousins had come to Prince Edward Island to fulfill their dreams. The Kuepfers and their cousin Mark Yutzy had bought farms, while their other cousin Mattie Kuhns ran the Celtic Knoll Farm Shop in a Quonset hut on the road along Shushan Bay. They, along with the rest of the community, would keep Juan's farm going, but for how long? She'd sold most of her herd and rented her larger fields after Boaz's death because she couldn't expect others to work on her farm forever. Would Juan have to do the same?

She bent her head to pray. Juan was going to need every prayer. As she closed her eyes, she couldn't see anything but his horrified face, shiny with petroleum jelly, when he realized he was blind. It was an image she'd never forget.

Wakening the next morning before the sun rose, Annalise wanted to believe yesterday's events had been a bad dream. She couldn't lose herself in denial. She'd offered to help, and she must. She paused to pray for her irascible neighbor.

Memories crowded the words, transporting her back to the barnyard yesterday. She'd called Juan's name over and over. She'd gotten an answer, but not the one she'd hoped for. The yap-yap-yap had belonged to Mei-Mei.

Annalise had kept the dog from running into the damaged area. With minuscule slivers of metal everywhere, the pug could have sliced her paws. Annalise had slipped a charred length of clothesline through Mei-Mei's collar and set the dog on the ground. The pug had pulled toward her left.

"Mei-Mei, behave!" she had ordered.

The dog had yanked the rope away.

"Wait!" Annalise had cried.

The dog had stopped and howled. In front of her was a crumpled form, facedown in the mud.

Juan! His clothing tattered and charred. She'd feared he was dead, but he wasn't. With God's grace, he'd survived the explosion.

Annalise sat on the edge of her bed and sighed. How was Juan doing after a night's rest? She could go over and ask. Lucas must have spent the night. How was

Lucas doing? Yesterday, he'd been so unlike his garrulous self. In fact, she couldn't remember a single time when he hadn't taken over any conversation, his enthusiasm giving him a chatty attractiveness that had endeared him to many of the community's young *maedels* before they realized he had no interest in a serious relationship.

Those Kuepfer brothers can't finish anything they start. How many times had Boaz said that?

She didn't want to add her grief with Boaz's death on top of the distress from yesterday. It was too much to think about before breakfast. She dressed and let the pug out in the yard before hurrying to the barn.

The damp grass beneath her feet was familiar, a haven in the midst of her storm of emotions. She took a steadying breath and let it sift out. It helped, and her heart no longer hammered against her chest.

As she reached the barn, she glanced at Juan's farm. The lights she'd seen in his barn every morning since February weren't on.

She milked the Guernsey, Mocha, and turned her out into the meadow with the four heifers. She cleaned the barn before heading to the house with the bucket of strained *millich* to begin breakfast. If she were smart, she'd let Mocha dry up and buy *millich* at the farm shop. She kept milking because Evie and *Grossmammi* Fern, her late husband's *grossmammi*, preferred raw *millich*.

She walked past the workshop where she kept her woodworking tools. It'd been too many weeks since she'd had a chance to make the wooden boats and animals she sold to tourists who visited Prince Edward Island in the summer. A few had already come to buy, and she hadn't had much selection. She should get back to the work she loved, but each time she considered going out to the workshop, she was distracted by other tasks.

A light came on in Juan's barn. Who was milking his cows this morning? Lucas or someone else?

She hurried into the house and tried to push Juan's face from her mind as she made porridge and toast and bacon. She spooned *kaffi* into the percolator and set it on the stove. Soon its aroma was weaving through the scents of salty, smoky bacon sizzling in the cast-iron pan. The sound of two footfalls upstairs announced her four-year-old daughter and *Grossmammi* Fern were ready to eat. Also, she was sure, ready to quiz her more about what had happened yesterday.

"Gute mariye, Mamm," she heard before small arms were flung around her in an enthusiastic hug. A small white cane with a red band and a mushroom tip brushed her leg.

Annalise gathered her sweet daughter to her. Evie was growing more every day. She was no longer a *boppli* or a toddler, but a little girl. Her fine blond hair refused to stay in a bun or braids. Her hazel eyes, a combination of Annalise's brown ones and Boaz's sea blue, sparkled. They didn't do much else, because her beautiful four-year-old daughter couldn't discern anything, not even the difference between darkness and light.

Annalise had, at first, been sad when she thought of Evie's future, though she knew Evie would always have support within the community. Evie astounded her anew every day. Working with therapists and teachers since shortly after her birth, Evie already knew how to read and write braille. She moved easily through the house and around the farm, using her cane and her other senses.

Would Juan learn to do the same?

She pushed him out of her head. "Did you want to help me pour the *kaffi*, *liebling*?"

Evie's nose wrinkled. "Yuck!"

Laughing, Annalise teased, "What are we going to do with you, Jolly-Jelly-Evie-Belly?" She used the name she'd given her *boppli* days after she was born. "You don't like anything but baking. You'd better find a husband who cares more about cakes than a clean house."

"Don't wants a husband." The little girl crossed her arms over her black apron and dress that were miniatures of Annalise's. "Wants a pony."

"I know." Annalise kept her voice light and her face averted, though Evie couldn't see her expression.

The idea of her daughter riding a temperamental pony made her shudder. Annalise couldn't be overprotective, but she also couldn't be reckless.

Boaz's *grossmammi* Fern came into the kitchen, leaning on her own cane. As always, she looked as neat as the pins keeping her dark green dress closed and her *kapp* on her white hair. She was bent from hard work and her movements slow and stiff, but her mind was active.

Greeting the other woman with a kiss and what she hoped didn't sound like fake cheerfulness, Annalise put breakfast on the table. She was surprised by how reticent her family was about what had happened at Juan's farm. Why weren't they peppering her with questions?

As they bowed their heads for silent grace, Annalise reached out to take her daughter's hand. She prayed for each of them as she did at every meal and added a quick prayer for Juan's recovery. Raising her head, she squeezed Evie's hand, their signal to begin eating.

Annalise was reaching for her spoon when the door opened. "Bishop Rodney!" She stood. *"Gute mariye."*

Rodney Wolfe, who was close to *Grossmammi* Fern's age, was bald. His long, white beard reached to the middle of his chest, but he had the strong shoulders of a man half his age. His hands were scarred from work, and his clothes, except on Sundays, carried the remnants of the smoke from his blacksmith's shop.

"Will you join us?" Annalise asked.

He waved for her to sit. "No reason for you to let your breakfast get cold. I've already eaten, but if you don't mind, I'll have a cup of your delicious *kaffi.*"

The conversation was lively while Annalise ate, though she didn't taste anything. Why was the bishop calling? It must have to do with Juan's accident, but why was he here instead of next door? She noticed Rodney and *Grossmammi* Fern switched the subject if Evie mentioned the explosion.

"*Danki* for the *wunderbaar* cup of *kaffi,*" Rodney said as he pushed back his chair. In an offhand tone, he asked, "Could I have a few minutes of your time, Annalise?"

She nodded and stood, too. When *Grossmammi* Fern showed a decided lack of curiosity, Annalise's own was piqued. Did the older woman know what the bishop intended to say?

The bishop, like the *doktor* the day before, motioned for Annalise to come with him. She did, and he led the way onto the porch. He walked to where her cows grazed. She followed, pausing by the fence when he did.

"I assume you know why I'm here," Rodney said.

"No."

"Juan Kuepfer was blinded yesterday."

"I know. I found him." She shivered, this time at the horrible memories.

The bishop nodded. "I came to ask you to help Juan learn what he must."

"Me?"

"It's the obvious solution," Rodney said. "You've helped Evie. You know what to do."

"Evie has had therapists and other professionals teaching her."

"So will Juan, once the *doktors* have completed their tests and are sure his sight won't come back. For now… You can give him a head start. There are others among the *Leit* who will assist, but you're the only one who can share what you've been taught for Evie."

The bishop was right, and if it had been anyone other than Juan Kuepfer, they wouldn't be having this discussion. She would have already volunteered. Making meals wasn't enough. God had put her in this time and this place for a reason. She had the skills Juan needed.

"He's a member of the *Leit*," the bishop said, warning she'd been lost in her thoughts too long. "It's our duty to care for one another as God cares for us."

"I know."

"So you'll help?"

"*Ja.* Of course." She hoped she wouldn't come to regret that answer.

Chapter Two

Juan was bored. It'd been three days since the explosion, and he was so bored he yearned to shout it to the world. Other than a brief but exhausting visit to the hospital where they'd x-rayed him and poked him and asked him a bunch of questions, coming to the same diagnosis of a concussion, he hadn't been out of his room. He was accustomed to taking care of his animals, tending to his fields, finishing the work on his house.

Walking the few steps from his bed to the rocking chair by the window had sapped him and made his head spin until he was afraid he'd throw up. He wanted to figure out what had happened and make sure his animals weren't traumatized. One of his horses, Lady, was supersensitive to noise. He tried to recall how loud the explosion had been.

He couldn't remember.

Other than pain, he couldn't remember anything about the explosion. He wouldn't have known something had exploded if Lucas hadn't mentioned it.

What had exploded?

That, his brother had answered when bringing him breakfast that morning. Juan had been reconstructing an old steam tractor. Somehow pressure had built in the tank. The explosion had sent boiling water across the barnyard. His animals had sensed danger and fled in time.

So now he sat and fought his unsteady stomach and tried not to touch his burned face and arms as questions rumbled through his battered brain.

When would he be able to see?

How could he farm when he couldn't walk across his room?

Why now?

The words rang through his aching head. The last was a *dumm* question. There wasn't any *gut* time to lose his sight. He'd spent the morning, while trying to puzzle out what had gone wrong, struggling to catch any glimpse of light.

The bedroom door opened, and his brother said, "Annalise is here."

"Why?" Startled, he sat straighter. A big mistake. His stomach cramped, and he swallowed hard to keep from embarrassing himself.

"Rodney sent her to help you. She's been guiding Evie. He thought she could help you, too, so you can get around while you're blind."

He clenched his hands. *Blind!* He already loathed the word. It was a label that announced he was somehow less. He'd never imagined a single word could send ugly rage through him. He didn't want to spend the rest of his life in darkness. Why had God let this happen?

"Tell her to go home," he growled.

"I can't." Lucas's voice hardened. "Rodney asked her to work with you. Are you going against the bishop's decision?"

"He doesn't know the whole story."

"No?" He guessed his brother was raising his eyebrows. He'd seen Lucas make that motion many times. "What whole story are you talking about?"

Juan didn't reply. Boaz had told him in confidence about his troubles with his wife and how she refused to support his dreams. How she'd tried to convince his *grossmammi* to side with her, how she always insisted on her way, even with the most mundane things. Listing her shortcomings seemed petty.

She's heeded the bishop's request to help you when she has every reason not to, his conscience reminded him. He wasn't sure if she believed it was Juan's fault Boaz had died. It didn't matter because Juan believed that enough for both of them.

"All right," Lucas said. "If you don't want to tell me, tell her. I'm sending her in."

Juan opened his mouth to protest, but heard his brother's steps leaving. He'd been told vision-impaired people's other senses became more fine-tuned. How long would that take? Today, other than his vision, his senses were the same as they'd been before the explosion.

Or maybe that wasn't true, because the scent of roses wafted into the room. Annalise. A memory triggered the image of her, her blond hair, her dark eyes, her long fingers. He'd never met a plain woman who used woodworking tools and sold her creations. As Boaz had complained several times, Annalise wasn't like other women.

"*Gute nammidaag*, Juan," Annalise said, her voice calm.

It was afternoon?

He appreciated she spoke softly, but he doubted her

serenity was real. His wasn't. "I know what you're doing here."

"Rodney requested I help you."

"Which means you don't want to be here."

She equivocated as he would have done if their situations were reversed. "We're a community. We help one another when and how we can."

He heard a rustle and guessed she'd removed her bonnet and set it on his dresser. A faint breeze came from her motions, and he heard her heel hit the chest at the foot of his bed as she sat.

"What if I don't want your help?" he asked, turning his head, though it was useless. The darkness in front of his eyes hadn't changed a bit, and it wouldn't until the bandages were removed.

"What will you do, then? Stay in your room until you grow old and die?"

"Don't be ridiculous. The *doktor* says I should have my sight back within six weeks. He's making an appointment for me in Charlottetown with a neurologist to make sure everything is as it should be."

"I don't want to burst your optimistic balloon, but having your sight back in six weeks isn't what Dr. Armstrong said."

"I heard what he said."

"Are you sure?"

He was about to fire back an answer, but faltered.

"No, I'm not sure of anything." His voice cracked on the last word.

A glass was thrust into his hand. He wrapped his fingers around it. He started to raise it to his lips, then lowered it.

"Don't think about what you're doing," Annalise said

in the soothing voice she'd used before. "Let your muscles do what they're used to doing."

"I can't see what I'm doing." He hated how petulant he sounded. How weak and useless.

"You must have had a drink of water in the middle of the night. You wouldn't have been able to see what you were doing, ain't so?"

She was right. He took a sip, not splashing any. She'd filled the glass halfway to give him a chance at success.

Be careful. He must not forget Boaz's comments about her pigheaded determination to do everything her way and how her temper flared when that didn't happen.

"More?" she asked when he'd drained the glass.

"I'm fine. *Danki.*" Trying to determine where she was because he'd lost track of her location, he turned to his right toward the painted chest at the foot of the bed. "I know I have to be patient and wait for my sight to return."

"Why not learn skills to help now?"

He heard the small bump of her shoe against the chest again and congratulated himself at guessing where she was. "Isn't it a waste of time?"

"Yours or mine?"

"Yours. You've got a house and a business as well as your farm." He couldn't keep bitterness out of his voice. "Me? I've got too much time on my hands."

"So let's put it to *gut* use."

Why did she have to be contrary and cheerful at the same time? "I'm trying to think of you."

"*Grossmammi* Fern has the house in hand." She stood, her dress and apron brushing the chest with the soft rustle of corn leaves being pushed aside as he walked through his fields.

When would he be able to do that again?

As if he asked that question aloud, Annalise said, "There's no reason to hide here. You should be thanking God you have a bungalow. You don't have to worry about stairs inside, though you'll need to handle the steps outside."

"Annalise, I don't want your help."

Another rustle. Was she folding her arms in a stubborn pose?

"Really?" she asked, her voice icy. "Did you get to that chair on your own?"

She was as vexing as Boaz had bemoaned.

"Well, did you?" she persisted when he didn't answer.

"Lucas helped me." The words were bitter on his tongue.

"He can't be here to help you every second of every day and every night." She paused, then said, "It's no different from your cousin Daisy having to learn to get around in a wheelchair."

"I know." His younger cousin had never acted discouraged about being confined to a wheelchair after an accident that left her partially paralyzed. Not that Daisy would call it "confined." Somehow, she found a way to get everywhere she wanted to go.

"I know you know, but I also know you don't want to remember how a little girl overcame so much. You'd rather molder away in this room feeling sorry for yourself."

His hands clenched on the rocker's arms. "Enough!"

"I agree. You need to learn to get around on your own. Why are you hesitating?"

Her composed voice exasperated him. "Because you are—" He halted. Nobody wanted to be described as pushy or bossy. Both words had burst into his mind.

"I'm what?" Annalise's voice suggested nothing he said or did would perturb her. "The last person in the world you'd want to be here?" She didn't give him a chance to answer. "Arguing is a waste of time, Juan. As you said, I don't have time to waste. I told Rodney I'd help you, and I'd appreciate it if you'd allow me to do so."

Juan was taken aback. Lost in his bewilderment and grief and rage, he hadn't stopped to realize how difficult the whole situation must be for her as well. When she'd come to collect the pug last time, he'd seen how she couldn't wait to be done with him. He hadn't been welcoming, but he suspected the reason she wanted to hurry away had been something more. Something deeper. Something far more painful.

They had one thing in common: the loss of her husband and his friend. Though Boaz had described her as headstrong, his friend couldn't hide his love for his wife. What would Boaz think of him, getting into a quarrel over petty details? Guilt overwhelmed him. If he'd been on the boat the day Boaz died, could Juan have saved his friend's life? Only God knew. Juan understood, but it didn't keep grief from trailing him.

"All right," he said.

"All right?" she repeated. "Does that mean you'll let me help you and teach you as I have Evie?"

"Ja."

"Gut," Annalise said, but he heard no satisfaction in her answer. "We'll start tomorrow morning."

"So soon?" His mouth tightened. "It might be better to wait until my head stops spinning each time I move."

"Then why are you sitting in a rocking chair? It must be making you feel terrible."

He was surprised when a rusty laugh creaked out of him. "That's a *gut* question."

"So you've been sitting there feeling sick to your stomach?"

"*Ja*. Not too smart of me, ain't so?"

"Definitely not smart of you." Her breath warmed his cheek, and he realized she was bending toward him. The aroma of roses swept over him, adding to his dizziness. She grasped his hands and tugged. "Put your feet beneath you and stand."

"I shouldn't. I could knock you down."

"I know how to balance you." A chuckle so quiet he almost missed it lightened her voice. "Besides, it wouldn't be the first time I've gotten bumped off my feet. Trust me. I learned how to do this with Evie."

"Who is much smaller than I am."

She pulled on his hands. "*Komm mol*, Juan. Give it a try. What can it hurt?"

He could have given her a long answer, but she was determined to get him on his feet. Doing as she instructed, he stood. He wobbled, but her hands gripped his, keeping him from falling.

"Okay?" she asked.

"I think so." He concentrated on how silken her skin was as she put her hands to his wrists. If he kept his mind on her fingers instead of how a task like standing shouldn't have been so difficult, he might be more stable.

Her hands were soft and as gentle as if he were a newborn *boppli*.

He could trust her to do as she'd promised. No more, but no less. He should let her help until he could see. That would fulfill the bishop's request.

She lifted his right hand and put it on her arm above the elbow. "When you're ready, let me know, and we'll get you to bed."

"Me ready? Aren't you going to help me?"

"I'm going to *guide* you. If I hold on to you, I could throw you off-balance."

The thought of holding her instead raced through his head. He ignored the tantalizing thought. His brain must be hurt worse than he'd guessed, if he was having thoughts about his friend's widow.

When Juan said he was ready to move, Annalise edged forward. He copied her motion, keeping the distance between them the same. He didn't stumble as she led him around the chest and to the side of his bed. She urged him to keep his hand on her arm as he sat. He released her and swung his legs onto the bed.

"Now the covers," she said.

"I don't know where they are."

"Do as you'd do in the middle of the night. Evie says her best tools are often her toes."

He swept his foot down the bed, pausing when he encountered the folded quilt and sheet. Reaching down until he could touch the bedding, he pulled it toward him.

"Excellent!" Annalise sounded pleased, too. "You should rest. I'll be here tomorrow. It isn't going to be easy."

"At least, it's only six weeks. Maybe less before my vision is back."

"Is that…?" Hesitation filled her voice for the first time. "Is that what you think Dr. Armstrong said?"

"Ja."

"That's not what he said, Juan."

"I heard him, and…" So many memories were gone, and the ones remaining were as rickety as an old fence gate. He wasn't sure which he could trust. Taking a deep breath, he asked, "So what did the *doktor* say?"

"He said it may take six weeks for any eyesight to return, that's true." A gentle undertone drifted into her voice. "He also said if you didn't regain any vision by that time, you may not ever." She patted the covers by the side of the bed. "I'm sorry."

A darkness that had nothing to do with his lost vision rolled over him as she walked out and closed the door, shutting him in with the truth. He sat and stared at his future…and saw nothing.

How was she supposed to help Juan when he didn't want her help? Annalise's hands clenched on the laundry basket she was carrying into the yard. The hanging clothes needed to be folded. She was glad to have something to do, something requiring her to focus her attention. She kept thinking of Juan's face when she revealed what Dr. Armstrong had said. If she'd realized Juan wasn't aware of the *doktor*'s dire words, she would have phrased things differently. Or she would have found a way to slip out of the room and let his brother break the appalling news to him.

She'd made a mess of everything. If she could start over, she would have kept the conversation from heading in that direction. Then she wouldn't have to figure out a way to face him tomorrow and apologize.

She was sorry. Sorry Juan Kuepfer had moved next door three months ago. He'd lived at his brother's house, a kilometer along the road that followed the wide Brudenell River. It paralleled Shushan Bay on the other side of the peninsula. Far enough so she didn't have to see him often, whether she wanted to or not.

God, give me patience to deal with my neighbor. I know he was Boaz's friend, and he's a member of our community, but if there's a way to keep our encounters from being so uncomfortable, please help me find it.

The answer wasn't selling the farm as *Grossmammi* Fern continued to urge her to do. She knew if she did, she would have the money to return her small family to Ontario where her parents and six siblings and their spouses lived. Her daughter, Evie, would have cousins to play with every day.

Annalise hadn't been logical and sold the farm. Boaz had brought them to Prince Edward Island because he'd believed their future was here. The farm was a legacy he'd wanted for her and Evie. He'd told her that before leaving for long hours away from them.

She sighed at the familiar frustration inside her. She wished now—as she had before Boaz died—that he'd spent more time with them. Family was more important than the things Boaz wanted to buy. They'd quarreled the night before he died. She'd never had a chance to apologize for her harsh words.

"Need help?" called *Grossmammi* Fern as she crossed the yard.

"I can manage." She smiled at the elderly woman who was trailed by her beloved pug.

"Then I'll stand here and chat with you while Evie naps. She fell asleep on the sofa." *Grossmammi* Fern leaned on her cane. "You've been quiet. What's troubling you?"

Everything, she wanted to say. Instead she said, "Juan is reluctant to let me help him."

"Will he cooperate?"

"*Ja*, because of the bishop's order." She started to place the towel on top of others in the basket, then realized there weren't any others yet. No wonder *Grossmammi* Fern had come out to see what was wrong.

Annalise must have looked silly doing nothing by the clothesline.

They talked a while longer, then *Grossmammi* Fern and Mei-Mei went back into the house. Annalise glanced at Juan Kuepfer's farm. In his last weeks, Boaz had been with his friend more than at home. They'd been repairing equipment, and Boaz had insisted it was absolutely necessary for him to help Juan. Not because Juan was his friend, but because Boaz was learning valuable mechanical skills he'd need once he bought a lobster boat.

"Why couldn't you be satisfied with being a farmer?" she whispered through clenched teeth. "Why did you want to become a lobsterman?"

She didn't get an answer. She didn't expect one. Boaz couldn't explain when he was alive, so she was *dumm* to think she'd find the answer after he'd died. Why hadn't she asked the question, before he went on his final trip, if he was trying to escape his life with her and Evie?

Chapter Three

The next day, Juan woke when he heard someone come into the house. He glanced at the windup clock on his nightstand, then grumbled under his breath when he realized he couldn't see anything. This was ridiculous! The *doktor* had said his eyes were undamaged, so why wouldn't they work?

Juan had asked that question last night when the *doktor* came to change the pads over his eyes. Dr. Armstrong had said that more tests would be done in Charlottetown soon.

"Don't expect instant answers," the *doktor* had said. "With brain injuries, finding answers can take time."

Time... That was all Juan had. Time filled with nothing but imagining a bleak future. If he couldn't do chores and handle fieldwork, he'd have to sell his farm. He thought of how many times he'd heard people mention it might be better if Annalise sold her farm because it was too much for her to handle. Already she had responsibility for a *kind* who was sightless. He refused to let the word *blind* form in his head. He'd agreed she should sell, because he'd hoped not having her next door would ease his guilt. He had to wonder what people were saying about him keeping his farm.

Dunnerwetter! Juan had never figured out how his *grossdawdi*'s favorite word that meant "thunder-weather" had anything to do with a nail that wouldn't go in straight or a cow that kicked. Now he understood. Saying the word eased the pressure crushing him.

Juan struggled to sit. Dizziness swooped on him like a dark cloud of bats, but subsided. The spinning stopped, and memories burst through his mind as if a dam had broken.

He examined each, savoring it and knowing he wouldn't take them for granted. The only moments he couldn't recall surrounded the explosion. It was as if those had been blown out of his head.

God, danki *for their return*, he prayed. He was glad to give up a few hours of memories to have the rest. This had to be a *gut* sign for his recovery.

If only he could see…something!

Footfalls came toward him. Annalise? No, something was swishing across the floor.

He started to ask who was there, but winced as something struck his bed. The faint tap sent a thud through his skull.

"Watch where you're going!" he snapped.

"I am." The voice was so young he wondered if the whole thing was a dream. He'd been having doozies since the explosion. It was as if his brain were trying to fill the voids in his memory by dumping a bizarre mixture of people and events into his dreams.

"You bumped my bed."

"Dids not. My cane dids."

"Your cane?" He frowned, then wished he hadn't when the motion made his head ache more. A cane held by someone with a young voice? "Are you Annalise's daughter?"

"*Ja*. My name's Evie Fern Overgard, and I'm four years old. This many old." She put four fingers on his arm, shocking him that she knew where he was. He'd been told she couldn't see anything. How could she know where he was when he was lost in a whitish-gray fog? Maybe the color of the fog was a *gut* sign. He'd assumed sightless people saw nothing but black.

"You're Juan, ain't so?" the *kind* continued.

Instead of answering the obvious, he asked, "What are you doing here?"

"I'm here to learns you." From her tone, he could almost see the tilt of her chin. A pert chin, as he recalled, like her *mamm*'s. Her whole face appeared from his memories. She was cute, resembling her *mamm* more than Boaz. Had she inherited his friend's easygoing ways? He hoped so, because he didn't want to deal with two stubborn Overgard females who thought they knew what was right for him.

No wonder he hadn't recognized her voice. He'd made every effort to avoid Annalise and her family at church services. Not that it'd been difficult, because Annalise seemed as eager to keep distance between them.

Odd that Boaz had never brought his daughter with him to visit Juan. His friend had seldom spoken of his *kind*. They'd talked about everything else. Each time Juan had brought up Boaz's family, his friend had changed the subject.

"Evie, where are you?" Annalise's voice drifted into the room, breaking him free from uncomfortable thoughts.

"With Juan, *Mamm*," the *kind* called.

"Shh." Her *mamm* came into the room, bringing the scent of roses with her. "Juan's head must hurt."

Had that been revealed by his expression? He needed to keep his expression neutral when Annalise was around. She didn't miss much.

"*Gute mariye*, Juan." Annalise's voice was soft. Did she always sound like that?

He hadn't let her say much when she came to collect *Grossmammi* Fern's runaway pug. When had he spoken to her before that? He couldn't recall, but not because his memory was elusive. He must have said something to her at Boaz's wake or funeral.

Hadn't he?

He remembered offering his sympathies to *Grossmammi* Fern, but not to Annalise. Had his guilt at the part he'd played in Boaz's death kept him silent? Lucas had reassured him plenty of times, saying Juan shouldn't blame himself for not being on the boat when Boaz went missing. That hadn't changed anything. Guilt had continued to hammer at Juan day after day until its constant pounding had become as familiar as his heartbeat.

"Are you ready to get started?" Annalise's question reminded him that he hadn't returned her greeting. Yet, she sounded cheerful.

Juan wished he could see her expression. Frustration seeped into his voice. "To do what?"

"I thought we'd start with basics."

"Like getting dressed and out of bed? Is that why you're here so early?"

"Early? It's almost 11:00 a.m."

Shock riveted him, and he turned toward the window, though he couldn't see the sunshine. "Really?"

"*Ja*. The *doktor* said you'd be sleeping more than usual while you heal. Don't worry. Your cows have been milked and your animals fed. Lucas has taken your horses and mules over to his farm so he can keep them exercised while he's working his fields."

"My fields—"

"Don't worry," she said. "Rodney has arranged for everyone to take a turn working here for as long as it's necessary."

The mattress moved, and Evie announced, "Time for lessons. That's what *Mamm* always says. Time for lessons."

"What lessons?" he asked. "Not how to get dressed or shaved, I assume."

"No." Something in Annalise's voice told him she was blushing. "I've already discussed with Lucas how to help you with that."

"Without cutting my throat?"

"That is one of the goals."

He chuckled. What was it about Annalise that teased him to laugh in the midst of disaster? She wasn't the woman he'd thought she was based on Boaz's descriptions. Or was he seeing another side of her relentless resolve? She was pleasant, but that might change if he resisted her efforts to do as the bishop had instructed.

"Let's start with something easy." Annalise put an object in his hand. "What's this?"

Juan rolled what felt like a wood cylinder between his fingers. It had no distinguishing marks except a knot near the top.

"I don't know," he said. "If it's a toothpick, it's a little wide."

Giggles rose from where Evie was sat beside him. "Don't be silly, Juan! *Mamm* mades these so I could learns to count." She stretched across him and patted his cheek as if to make sure his face was aimed in her direction. She touched his features lightly as if mapping them, then asked, "Do you knows how to count?"

"As high as my fingers and toes will allow."

The little girl giggled, and the sound sent unexpected warmth through him. He hadn't spent much time around young *kinder*. He was the last born in his family, and three of his brothers and his five sisters had left their community in Ontario. Some had moved west, some had gone to other districts in Ontario, and two had decided not to be baptized and lived in the United States. Then he and Lucas had moved to Prince Edward Island. Their next older brother, Willis, had remained to take over *Daed*'s roofing business. None of his siblings had had *kinder* before they left home.

"Evie," Annalise said, "there is a glass of *millich* and two cookies on the table. Let me get Juan started on this, and later you can help him practice so he can get as *gut* as you."

"Okays." The bed bounced as the little girl slid off.

He heard an unfamiliar swish as Evie left the room. He wanted to ask what it was, but Annalise preempted his question.

"Are you ready, Juan?"

"As ready as I'll ever be. Are you going to teach me shapes?"

"That's not the lesson." She handed him a square piece of wood that was about five centimeters on each side and two and a half centimeters thick. "Go ahead. Examine it."

He ran his fingers around the wood. It was flat on what he assumed was the bottom, but it had three shallow holes drilled in the top.

"Put the peg in the middle hole," she ordered in the same unruffled voice.

Juan almost laughed. What *gut* would it do? He should be able to manage that with his eyes closed.

He couldn't. He kept trying to poke the peg into the hole, but it wouldn't go in, either because he didn't have it straight or it glanced off the side. Finally he managed to get it into the hole.

"Wrong one," Annalise said. "Try again."

When she plucked the cylinder out and handed it to him, he shook his head. "This is a waste of time. I told you I don't want—I don't need your help. I'm supposed to rest, not play stupid games. You've done your *gut* deed, so why don't you leave me alone?"

"Being angry won't help."

"I'm not angry," he retorted, though he was. Angry, frustrated, fearful of what the future would be. Everything he attempted to do showed how much his life had changed, and he didn't know how to fix it. "I'm… I'm…"

He'd thought she would fill in the blank, but she remained silent. The faint sound of her breathing told him she was there. She hadn't stormed off nor had she chided him for his outburst. Instead, she'd waited while he'd spewed his bile.

Making this patient woman match the stories Boaz had told him about Annalise's short fuse and strong will was impossible. Had the whole world gone topsy-turvy?

Though she longed to say something comforting to Juan, Annalise bit back the words. They would infuriate him more, but he needed to try for as many times as it took him to learn to put the peg in the proper hole.

Those Kuepfer brothers can't finish anything they start. Boaz's words whispered in her mind. That might be so, but she couldn't let Juan quit before he'd begun.

Folding her arms, she asked, "Are you going to try again?"

"Do I have any choice?"

"You always have a choice," she replied, glad to hear his fury had sifted away.

"To try or not?"

"*Ja.* That choice and many others."

"What other choices do I have when I can't take a step without being so dizzy I feel like I'm going to fall on my nose?"

Sympathy rushed through her, but she knew better than to express it. So many times, Evie had tried to convince her that something was impossible because her daughter didn't want to work on mastering the skill. It had hurt her heart to insist then, but soon Evie had learned and was moving on to the next challenge.

"You have the choice to laugh. It's a better choice than crying, ain't so?" She hurried on when she saw his brows lower. She wished she could reach out and smooth the lines from his forehead above the gauze over his eyes, but that might add to his pain. "Or maybe I should have said 'sulking' because men don't like to admit crying may be the best choice."

"Are you trying to start a quarrel?"

"Of course not!" She stepped away as if Juan had slapped her.

He had. Not with his hand, but with his words.

He must have realized how sharp his response had been because he said in a more normal tone, "Lucas and I were talking. The explosion must have been caused by the steam tractor."

"The one you and Boaz were rebuilding as a stationary engine for your dairy tank?"

He nodded. "When I bought the farm, the tractor was

stored in a tumbledown shed. I debated for a couple of months whether I should try to repair it or strip it down for parts. Boaz was eager to work on it, and we spent a lot of time on it before…before the other accident."

Feeling heat climbing her cheeks, she looked away, relieved he couldn't see her face becoming a brilliant crimson. She should have set ground rules before they began working together. All they needed was a single one: no talking about Boaz or the accident that had taken his life.

Did Juan feel the same disquiet? He changed the subject by saying, "I need to ask you a question."

"I'll be glad to answer while you put the peg in the middle hole."

The faintest of smiles tugged at his lips. "Always the taskmaster, I see."

"It's for your own *gut*."

Annalise thought he might retort, but instead he said, "Evie checked to make sure my face was tilted toward her. Why does that matter when neither of us can see the other?"

"Evie is aware of how sighted people interact. She realizes people pay more attention to what she's saying if they're looking at her."

"Why does it matter when I can't *look* anywhere?"

A vulnerable expression crossed his face. Not pain. She'd seen that often since the explosion. Was it puzzlement? Uncertainty? She couldn't guess, but she sensed it was one he wouldn't have wanted her to see.

"That's something only you can answer, Juan. I'm here to help you gain the basic skills you need."

"By putting a peg in a hole?"

"It's about training your fingers to be sensitive. Without your eyes, you have to depend on your other senses.

Contrary to what you may have been told, your other senses don't become more whetted when you lose one. You have to learn to heed them."

"By putting a peg in a specific hole?"

"That's a start," she said. "We depend on sight more than our other senses."

"I'm seeing that." He grimaced as the peg fell onto the floor. "Pun not intended."

"Don't worry about using words like *see* or *look*. You being anxious about them will make others uncomfortable." She handed him the peg. "If someone calls to you from outside the barn, you know who it is by the voice, ain't so?"

"*Ja.*"

"If that same person is in the barn with you and calls, what do you do?"

"I don't know what you mean."

"Don't you turn to face that person?"

He nodded. "It's the polite thing to do."

"*Ja*, it's polite, but it's also because we've learned to be dependent on sight to confirm what we already know." She watched as he struggled to put the peg in the correct hole. "I'm going to leave you to work on that peg. All right?"

"*Ja.*"

She'd never heard such a reluctant *ja*. No, that wasn't true. She'd sounded the same when she agreed to Rodney's request. Neither she nor Juan was happy about being thrown together.

For how long? The sooner she could help him learn simple tasks, the sooner she could be done with these sessions…and with the man who should have been by her husband's side on the last day of his life.

Chapter Four

Juan woke when something wet stroked his hand.

What trick was Lucas playing on him? How many times had his older brother pranked him before school?

That was Juan's first thought, but it was followed by the realization he'd finished school more than a dozen years ago. Why was he asleep in the middle of the day? The sun's warmth on his face told him it must be afternoon because his bedroom faced west.

The wet brushed his skin. What…?

He turned his head, then grimaced. Habit died hard, and he hadn't gotten it through his head in the past week that it didn't matter in which direction he looked. He saw the same dark grayness.

But at least Dr. Armstrong removed the gauze. His mental voice was too chipper this morning.

Warm, pungent breath struck his face.

A dog.

Had *Grossmammi* Fern's yippy little pug gotten into his house? Had Annalise brought the pest with her? Every step he took, even a week after the accident, was a challenge. If he tripped over the little dog…

Another lick from a wide tongue drenched his face.

That couldn't be Mei-Mei. It had to be a much bigger dog because he could feel its breath—and *smell* its breath. He stretched out his hand, and the dog pressed its broad head against his palm. In amazement, he discovered the dog's nose was level with his own.

A very big dog.

He leaned forward to run his hand along the dog's shoulders. Though he stretched as far as he could, his fingers didn't reach the dog's tail.

A *very, very* big dog.

And a friendly one because it licked his cheek, leaving a damp trail. Like a wave tumbling him head over heels in the ocean.

"How did you get in here, dog?" he asked.

From the doorway, he heard his brother reply, "I was about to ask that. Do you know, Annalise?"

Juan sat, ignoring his spinning head. At least he didn't get sick to his stomach each time he moved now. He wondered how long Annalise had been there, watching him. He hadn't heard her walk toward his room.

You didn't hear Lucas either, and you're not upset about that. He paid no attention to the reasonable voice in his mind. How many times had Boaz complained about his wife sticking her nose in where it didn't belong? Now she was doing that in Juan's life.

A sigh slipped past his lips. She wasn't sticking her nose into his life by choice. She didn't want to be there any more than he wanted her there.

Yet, he couldn't deny how dedicated she was. She came every morning before Lucas returned to his own chores after finishing Juan's. She never hurried away, though she must have so much to do. On sunny days, Evie came with her, but when it rained, she left her daughter at home with her great-*grossmammi*. Either she didn't want the little girl to get soaked or she preferred not to have to clean extra wet and muddy footprints in the house.

Annalise's voice broke into his thoughts. "I don't know how I could have missed a huge dog sneaking into the house. Can you open doors, doggie?"

"What kind of dog is it?" Juan asked.

"Saint Bernard," Lucas replied.

"Partly," Annalise corrected. "She doesn't look like a purebred. Not quite as big as others I've seen."

His brother chuckled. "Whatever she is, she's big. Do you need another draft horse, Juan?"

"Whose dog is it?" He turned toward Annalise. "You said you've seen other Saint Bernards?"

"In Ontario. Not here. I don't know where she's from." She paused, then said, "Too bad you can't talk."

Juan started to ask her what she meant, then realized she was speaking to the dog. There had been a gentleness in her voice that he'd heard only when she was talking to or about her daughter.

His brother said, "I saw her yesterday. I called, but she refused to approach me. I've asked, but nobody is missing a Saint Bernard."

"Half Saint Bernard, according to Annalise who's seen more of the breed." He regretted the sarcastic edge on his words. He hadn't meant to sound bitter.

"I think you're right, Annalise," Lucas said, his tone conciliatory. "She's got the face and jowls of a Saint Bernard, but she's no bigger than a small heifer." His brother snapped his fingers. "I've got a great idea! You should keep her, Juan."

"Keep her? She'll eat me out of house and home." This time he made sure to sound as if he were jesting.

He didn't want to acknowledge how he'd sunk every penny he had in the farm.

"She could help you get around."

"How? Do you expect to hook her to a pony cart?"

Lucas chuckled. "She's big enough, ain't so? I was thinking she could be one of those guide dogs."

Hope mixed with horror at the thought of having to depend on a dog. Juan had to recognize that with the dog he'd be able to navigate without smashing his nose or toes or everything in between by walking into a wall.

Before he could reply, Annalise said, "Lucas, I don't know if a Saint Bernard can be trained to be a guide dog. Canadian Guide Dogs uses golden or Labrador retrievers or a mix of the two breeds. In the United States, they also use German shepherds. I've never heard of a Saint Bernard being a guide dog."

"You know a lot about this," Juan said. "Have you considered one for Evie?"

"*Ja*, but a candidate must be sixteen years old before a dog will be matched to them." Her voice grew wistful. "Before we moved to Prince Edward Island, I wanted to foster puppies for Canadian Guide Dogs. They can't begin their guide training until they're a year and a half old, so before that they live with families who teach them about being around people and having *gut* manners."

"Did you foster one?"

"No."

"Why not?"

"Boaz didn't want me to."

He understood what she hadn't said. How many times had Boaz complained she spent too much time on things beyond her home and her family? He'd been aggravated about her woodshop.

A complete waste of time, Boaz had bemoaned while working on the tractor.

For the first time, Juan was pinched by empathy for her. He could hear how much she'd wanted to raise puppies to be trained as guide dogs, something that wouldn't have helped her daughter for years. Instead of supporting her generosity, Boaz had quelled it.

He'd always considered his friend to be single-minded, but he never had thought about what that would mean for Boaz's family. It'd been simpler to focus on rebuilding the tractor.

Knowing he'd be smart to keep his mouth shut, he couldn't keep from asking, "Why can't you take care of puppies here?"

"We're too far from the training centers." Her voice remained emotionless. "Canadian Guide Dogs likes to have foster families nearby."

"That makes sense." What didn't make sense was why Boaz would keep her from doing something that would have helped so many people. Had he worried she and Evie would become too attached to the puppies?

"Mamm?"

Juan heard the little girl's cane preceding her into the room. She walked with a confidence he had to envy. His few attempts to walk around his room had been humiliating. He'd lurched forward a few steps, then run into something.

"Evie…" began Annalise.

"He's here!" exclaimed the *kind.*

"Ja, Lucas and Juan are here."

"No, the dog is here."

"The dog is a girl."

"Oh. A girl dog? Like Mei-Mei?"

Lucas chuckled. "About ten times bigger than your great-*grossmammi*'s dog."

"I knows." Evie's grin didn't need to be seen. It was obvious in her words. "He—I means, she and I ares *gut* friends."

Annalise asked, "You know this dog?"

"*Ja.*"

"Do you know whom she belongs to?"

"*Ja.*"

"Who?"

"She belongs to herself, ain't so?"

The dog barked, a deep, resonating sound that must have been heard across the broad river.

With a patience he couldn't have emulated, Annalise asked, "Where have you seen the dog before?"

"When she and I talks on the porch."

"Did you let her into the house?" Juan asked, curious.

"*Ja*, I lets her in. She wants to see what's in the house. I opens the door. We comes in. I stops for a cookie." She gave a big sigh. "No cookies."

Juan heard Lucas's smothered laugh. He could envision Lucas's face contorting as he tried not to let the little girl discover how amusing he found her words. Juan might have as well if it hadn't been his house invaded by the gargantuan dog.

Then he realized it might not have been the worst thing. If Evie had left the big dog alone, the beast could have taken it into her head to chase the livestock. The cows and goats might have stood together against a large dog, but the sheep would have panicked. Who knows what the nitwitted creatures might have done? Run against the fence and hurt themselves? He enjoyed keeping sheep, but had said more than once that they were the most foolish creatures on God's green earth.

Evie had made the best decision she could have to protect his animals, even if that hadn't been her intention.

Lucas said, "As you don't need my help with that monster dog, I'll be on my way."

"Are you stopping in later?" Annalise asked before Juan could.

"I'll be back for supper. It'll have to be a quick one, Juan."

"You've got a date?"

His brother shrugged, but didn't deny it before he left. Juan would have been surprised if Lucas had said he wasn't meeting someone. Lucas almost always had a date. He liked to flirt, and the girls liked him doing that. That Lucas was the clichéd tall, dark and handsome made them forget he was a serial admirer. He never walked out with any girl more than once or twice. Yet, they acted as if they didn't mind, that they knew he'd put an end to the game of musical chairs and settle down.

Juan wasn't so sure. His brother had never paid attention to any girl since Robin Boshart in Ontario. That hadn't worked out, though Juan had no idea why, and the relationship ended about a year before Lucas urged them to relocate to Prince Edward Island.

Annalise left, along with Evie and the dog, and Juan guessed she had something to talk about with his brother. Annoyed because he was tired of being left out of discussions about his future, he got out of bed. He managed to find his boots because he'd left them by his bed as Annalise had suggested. Pulling them on, he had to appreciate all he'd already garnered from her lessons. However, his annoyance with Lucas and Annalise overshadowed his gratitude. He didn't want to be a bystander in his own life.

Or was it something else?

He paused as he was about to stand. Was his brother interested in Annalise for a different reason? She was attractive, and Lucas couldn't resist a pretty face. His brother laughed more when she was in the house. That lighter tone was a sure sign of interest.

Annoyance became something stronger, something Juan didn't want to examine. Better to leave it alone.

He took a single step toward the door, his fingers following the line of the mattress to guide him. He halted when a rush of motion came from his doorway. A bulk of fur and muscle bumped into him, almost knocking him off his feet. He grasped the footboard.

"Slow down!" Annalise's warning was a few seconds too late.

"We wants to visit Juan!" Evie patted his arm. "He needs friends."

"I do?" he asked, startled. "What gives you that idea?"

"Lucas says—"

Annalise interrupted, "It's not nice to repeat what others say. What did *Grossmammi* Fern tell you?"

"'Whoever talks about others will talk about you,'" the little girl said. "*Mamm*, I'm doing the talkings!"

"Evie, you need to let someone else have a turn to talk."

"Okays. Juan, it's your turn."

His head spun with the ping-pong conversation. He put up his hand to steady it, but was halted when a long lick left it wet.

"The dog's with you?" he asked.

"I'm not sure what else to do with her," Annalise replied. "I don't want her to go into the road and get hit. It would be… She's a sweet dog, ain't so?"

He didn't need to be able to see her glance at her

daughter to know where Annalise's concerns were. The *kind* had lost her *daed*, and Annalise wanted to protect her from more grief.

"She's a sweetie." Evie's voice was muffled, and he guessed she'd pressed her face into the dog's thick coat. "Her name is Susie."

"How do you know that?" he asked, astonished. If Evie knew the creature's name, she might know where the dog belonged.

"She tells me."

"She told you?"

She must have raised her head because her words were clear as she asked, "Why wouldn't a dog knows her name?"

That was a question he couldn't answer. Add it to the questions of when his eyesight would return and how he was going to deal with Annalise until then, and the question that wouldn't leave him alone: Why, if Boaz had a caring tight-knit family, had he avoided spending time with them?

Annalise bit her lip not to laugh at Juan's baffled expression. He wasn't accustomed to a four-year-old's imagination which was often as real to Evie as everything around her.

"Susie is a nice name," she said, putting her hand on her daughter's shoulder.

"Susie's a nice dog, and she wants a job." Evie's certainty warned she wouldn't be dissuaded. "She likes to work, and she likes me."

It was Annalise's turn to be confounded. How did her young daughter know a Saint Bernard was a working dog, accustomed to completing tasks? Sometimes, Evie's insight awed her.

"I can tell she likes you, *liebling*." She laughed when the dog lapped Evie's hand, leaving the little girl giggling, before the dog turned to give Juan a sloppy kiss on his arm. "And Juan. Jolly-Jelly-Evie-Belly, take Susie into the living room and tell her a story. She'll like the one about the three goats."

"Okey-dokey," her daughter chirped before leading the dog from the room.

Annalise watched them go. Had the dog had obedience training, or was she happy to be with someone who adored her as Evie did?

She drew in a silent breath before facing Juan. Lucas's words rang in her ears. *Juan is acting more listless every day. Like he's given up.* It was easy to slip into despair. Talking about how Boaz had refused to let her raise Canadian Guide Dog puppies had brought memories of how discouraged she'd become with Boaz's peculiar behavior. *Grossmammi* Fern had put her small foot down when Boaz had balked after a development program had been put together to ease infant Evie into a life among the seeing. He hadn't said why, but she knew. He was ashamed of Annalise and the *kind* she'd given birth to. Her hope that would change as he spent more time with Evie had been dashed when he did everything he could to avoid his daughter.

Shoving memories aside, she smiled at Juan, not caring he couldn't see it. The smile was as much for herself as it was for him.

"Annalise," Juan said, "I appreciate you coming over here each day, but I think it'd be an excellent idea for me to make my own meals from now on."

"Don't be absurd. You could get burned."

"I know not to touch something hot."

"You'll splash water. The next thing you'll know you'll slip and fall."

"I'm not a *boppli*, Annalise. Please don't treat me like one."

"Please don't act like one," she replied. "Don't try to run before you've relearned how to walk."

"How long's that going to take?"

Why did he ask her questions she had no answers to? "I could say it'll take as long as it must, but you don't want to hear that. So I'll say you need to have reasonable goals."

"Like what?"

"Learning to move through the house before you start preparing meals. You're steadier on your feet, so we'll begin that tomorrow."

His frown eased. "How long will that take?" He waved aside her words before she spoke. "*Ja, ja*, I know. As long as it must, but I need to get outside."

"Why?"

"To find out what happened." Honest pain scored each word. "To find out what exploded."

She searched his face, seeing his determination to escape his prison. "Wasn't it the old steam tractor? You told me it caused the explosion."

"Did I?" His brows lowered in a thoughtful frown, and she suspected he was searching his mind. "*Ja*, that makes sense. And I already told you that?"

"You did."

"My memory is almost as messed up as my eyes. I remember some things, and others have slipped away. There's no rhyme or reason to which ones. None of that is important."

"That your memory isn't reliable *is* important."

He waved aside her words as if she were no older

than Evie. "The *doktor* said my memory should return once the headaches start easing."

"I didn't know they were still plaguing you."

"It's because I can't sleep for more than an hour or two at a time." He groped for the chair beside his dresser.

She took his hand and guided him to sit on it, though she'd cautioned him over and over to hold on to her, not the other way around. It was important to reach out to him in his pain. To keep it from consuming him and drowning him in anger and resentment, as her frustration with Boaz had done to her.

Not now! she told those memories. She understood why Juan couldn't sleep. More nights than she wanted to count she'd stared at the dark ceiling and pondered what she'd done to alienate her husband. After his death, she'd lain awake as she longed to go back in time and convince him not to go out on that lobster boat.

"We were careful with each repair we made," Juan said, freeing her from the sticky clutches of regret. He leaned forward, resting his elbows on his knees. "The tractor was ancient, and I was careful when moving it over to Lucas's farm and then back here when I moved in. It hadn't been touched in years. We checked and rechecked each weld we made. I checked the ones Boaz made, and he checked mine. We wanted to avoid what happened, but we must have missed one."

"Maybe you didn't."

His head jerked up. "What do you mean? The tractor exploded! We had to have done something wrong."

"Maybe, maybe not. It may not have had anything to do with what you did. Or what you didn't do. It may have been metal fatigue or something like that."

"I didn't see any signs, but it could have been hidden beneath the rust."

Annalise wasn't sure if he was making a joke until he grinned. Something he should do more often. The expression rearranged the strained lines cutting into his face.

"That's something you can find out once you're getting around better," she said, then wished she hadn't when his frown returned. "Shall I bring you something to eat? I've got chicken corn noodle soup and hot roast beef sandwiches." She laughed. "Afterward, I'll take Susie to my place. I can put her in the barn. The cows are outside so she won't be a bother."

Both brows rose. "You want to take the dog with you?"

She almost said, *You can't take care of yourself. How do you think you can care for a dog?* She didn't. That would have been too cruel.

"I assumed you didn't want her here," she said instead.

"I don't, but you shouldn't have to shoulder the responsibility for her. What will your other dog do? She yips at everything. She'll go crazy if you bring another dog there."

"That's why I'm not bringing her into the house. I can't let her run free. Evie's already attached to her."

"Do you always give your daughter everything she wants?"

She recoiled from the unexpected venom in his question. Where had *that* come from?

"No," she said. "I'll return later with your dinner."

She didn't wait for his answer. She rushed out before he could say something more hurtful. Something as harsh as Boaz would have.

Chapter Five

Annalise was in an unsettled mood when she got up
the next morning. Her dreams had been a mishmash of
people and places and conversations that couldn't have
happened in real life, each scene more confusing than
the previous one. She shouldn't have been surprised.
Her life was a muddle, so why should her dreams be
any different?

She dressed and brushed her hair into its bun. After
pinning her conical *kapp* in place, she rushed downstairs. She made sure she skipped the third step from
the bottom, the one that had a tendency to screech when
the house was quiet. It didn't make the same obnoxious
sound during the day, and she hadn't figured out why.
Maybe it had to do with the humidity or the light from
a nearby window warming the wood.

Or maybe it wants attention.

Shaking the thought out of her head, she rushed to
do her morning chores. She paused long enough to give
Susie a pat on the head. Her plans to leave the dog in
the barn had come to naught. Her two attempts to close
the door with Susie inside had failed. The first time,
the dog had slipped past her. The second time, Susie

had begun to howl with so much heartbreak Annalise couldn't bear to leave her.

Hoping she wasn't making a big mistake, she'd put Susie in the meadow with the cows. She'd half expected to return from Juan's house and find the dog gone. Susie had been waiting for her and Evie, who declared Susie must sleep inside overnight. Giving in, Annalise thought of Juan's sharp comment, and she wished he'd been there when she refused to let Susie sleep in Evie's room. Instead, she'd put a worn quilt in the utility room. The dog had acted as if it were the nicest place she'd ever been given. Sorrow filled Annalise as she wondered if that were so.

She glanced at the ceiling and *Grossmammi* Fern's room above the kitchen, then opened the door to let the big dog go outside. If Susie ran away, it would break Evie's heart, but Annalise didn't have any way to leash her. Images played through her mind of the post holding the porch roof snapping in two if the dog tugged hard to escape.

When Susie dropped to the porch floor with what sounded like a sigh of contentment, Annalise headed to the barn. The morning was crisp, especially after the last few warm days. Her hopes of finishing quickly were banished when Mocha refused to enter the barn and leave the other cows. Finally Annalise had the cows join Mocha inside. She grimaced. It'd take longer to clean after five cows.

That thought spurred her to milk the cow swiftly, though she made sure she'd gotten every drip, not wanting Mocha to get an infection. The cows were as indecisive about going out as they'd been to come in. It took twenty minutes to get them outside and another half an hour to clean the barn.

Sorrow settled on her as she recalled the days before Evie was born when she and Boaz had worked together in the barn. They'd been a great team, having their separate tasks while enjoying time together. Everything had changed when Evie arrived and Annalise had to devote time to their *kind.* Boaz had grown resentful. She hadn't known if it was because she was spending less time with him or if he hated having to do more chores.

When Annalise got back to the house, she was surprised to see Boaz's *grossmammi* standing by the kitchen door.

"I didn't realize you were going to park a pony on the porch," *Grossmammi* Fern said, her lips twitching. She pulled her black sweater closer around her because the morning chill belied that it was spring.

"A pony on the porch?" Annalise asked, shocked. "You saw a pony on the porch? When?"

The older woman gave her a concerned glance as she opened the door so they could go inside. "No, not a pony. A big dog. I was making a joke. Or trying to…"

Annalise rubbed her fingers against her forehead. "Sorry. My brain has turned into a mosquito this morning. Buzzing in a dozen different directions and as irritating."

Grossmammi Fern filled a cup with steaming *kaffi* and shoved it along the counter toward Annalise. "Sounds like you need this more than I do."

"Danki." She let the enticing aroma waft over her face as she sat.

"You aren't surprised there's a dog on the porch." *Grossmammi* Fern poured another cup and sat across from Annalise.

Between sips, Annalise explained how the dog had inveigled her way into Evie's heart. She finished with,

"I can't cut the dog loose. Who knows what would happen to her?"

"What will happen to Evie if the dog's owners come to claim her?"

"It won't be easy, but I hope she'll see the right decision is returning Susie to her owners."

"Susie? Odd name for a dog."

With a soft chuckle, Annalise took another bracing sip. "Evie told us the dog informed her that was her name."

Grossmammi Fern smiled. "That *kind* is blessed with an amazing imagination."

"I'm not sure *blessed* is the right word, but she has quite the imagination."

Evie's arrival, eager for breakfast, changed the subject. Making sure her daughter ate eggs along with her favorite raisin-bread toast, Annalise listened to the little girl chat with her great-*grossmammi*. They planned to spend the morning baking, which would give Annalise time to work with Juan without her daughter's input. She'd seen how he became annoyed if Evie became impatient with his progress.

Washing the dishes after breakfast, Annalise was up to her elbows in suds as she rinsed out the tall percolator. Bubbles flew in every possible direction, including over her, when a shriek came from the porch.

"What's that?" cried Evie.

"I don't know." Annalise threw her dishrag into the sink and ran to the door. She threw it open.

"Look!" cried *Grossmammi* Fern.

She did, scanning the porch for a snake or a skunk. All she saw was the dog with her legs stretched out in front of her.

"Look!" *Grossmammi* Fern pointed a quivering finger at Susie, who was regarding them with a calm Annalise envied.

"I don't know what you want me to look at."

"She…" She choked. "She's eating kittens!"

"What?" Shock riveted Annalise. She'd trusted Susie with Evie.

"Look!"

Though she didn't want to, Annalise knelt by the dog. Susie's feathered tail swept the porch behind her as she gazed at Annalise with devoted eyes. Tiny kittens were caught beneath her wide jowls. Praying the dog wouldn't bite her, she slipped her hands under Susie's broad left jowl. She winced when liquid oozed along her hands. Was it blood from one of the poor kittens? She started to gag, then gasped when she heard a soft mew.

And another.

And yet another.

She pushed aside Susie's jowl. The dog continued to wag her tail, not bothered by Annalise's poking and prodding. Annalise pulled out a trio of kittens who regarded her with wide eyes. They mewed hungrily. Putting them on the floor, she watched as they crawled back under the dog's jowl, curling against Susie's jaw.

Annalise sat on her heels. "I think they're trying to stay warm." She laughed as she gathered the kittens again, this time putting them in her apron. "Poor *Mamm* Cat is going to have to clean off a lot of drool when she takes them back to the barn."

Grossmammi Fern shook her head. "I've never seen such a thing in my whole life."

Rising, Annalise brushed her hands down her apron, then grimaced. She'd spread dog slobber on herself.

"Sorry to think poorly of you." *Grossmammi* Fern extended a hand toward the big dog.

Susie sniffed it, and her tail thumped against the porch. It was clear *Grossmammi* Fern's apology had been accepted, and the dog wanted to be friends. Then her head snapped up.

Evie came onto the porch. On her heels was Mei-Mei. The black pug squared her legs and began barking as if she'd never seen another dog before. *Grossmammi* Fern scooped her up, the pug remaining stiff. The big dog cowered against the house, daunted by the pug.

"Sich ruhich," *Grossmammi* Fern ordered.

Mei-Mei ignored her, clearly not intending to be quiet.

"You two needs to be friends," Evie said. "You're sisters, and sisters haves to love each other. That's the rule, ain't so?"

"It is," said a deeper voice from behind Annalise.

She turned to see the bishop. Rodney smiled as he continued to speak to her daughter, "Jesus taught each of us to love all of us. It sounds simple, but it isn't always."

"I loves *Mamm*," Evie replied as Annalise set the kittens on the porch. They ran toward a ginger cat that appeared at the barn's door, yowling for them. "And I loves *Grossmammi* Fern and I loves Juan and his animals and I loves Mei-Mei and I loves Susie and I loves *Mamm* Cat and all her kittens she's got in the barn." She paused, then added with a grin, "And you, too, Bishop Rodney."

He chuckled. "I was wondering if I was included."

"Jesus saids all, and you're 'all,' too," she said as if he hadn't said that a few moments ago.

"Who is Susie?" the bishop asked.

As Evie began to explain how the dog had found them at Juan's farm and how she'd come home with them, Annalise was glad she hadn't had to answer. She wasn't sure if she could get words out without choking on each one.

Evie had listed everyone except her *daed*. Had she forgotten Boaz? Annalise tried to remember the last time her daughter had spoken of him without Annalise mentioning him first. She couldn't recall, but she must talk more to her daughter about Boaz. Letting Evie forget her *daed* would be appalling.

Though Boaz had been unhappy about the *Englisch* therapists who came to their house, he'd seldom missed tucking his daughter into bed with a story or a song. From the time she was born until the family came to Prince Edward Island, Boaz had savored that special time with his daughter. After they'd arrived on the Island, Boaz had missed his daughter's bedtime more and more until during his last months, he was gone every night.

When the bishop asked to speak to Annalise, *Grossmammi* Fern led Evie into the house to begin their daily baking. The vexed pug glared at the other dog and followed. Rodney patted Susie on the head and was rewarded by another wag of her tail and an enthusiastic lick that left his beard damp on one side.

He rubbed his hand against it. "She's used to people. I wonder where her owner is."

"Lucas said she showed up on his farm a couple of days ago."

"If her owners are around, they'll be found. It's not like someone could fail to notice when a seventy-pound dog goes missing." He rested his hand on the clapboards as he asked, "How are things going with Juan?"

"He still can't see anything, not even the difference between sunlight and shadow."

"That wasn't what I meant. I was asking how he's doing with adjusting to his blindness."

She wanted to say Juan was resisting every idea she had to help him, but she didn't. Juan had had a terrible accident and was living with the consequences. She shouldn't be judging him. She knew what it was like to suffer an appalling loss. Almost six months had passed since Boaz's body had been recovered after he went missing. The thought of those horrible hours of hoping and fearing and praying and anger sent shudders through her.

"What else is wrong, Annalise?" Rodney asked, proving how insightful he was. The lot had fallen on the right man when he was chosen as their bishop.

The smile she'd hidden behind so often slipped into place. "Too much to do in too few hours of the day."

"If you want me to find someone else to help Juan…"

She wanted to shout *Ja!* but said, "I'm glad to help him. Just complaining like always."

"You complain? Not that I've heard."

Because I keep it to myself. She silenced her honest response and shifted the conversation to which *Englisch* van service would be best when Juan went to the specialist in Charlottetown. It was a safe subject when so many others might lead to the truth deep in her heart: Boaz had longed to become a lobsterman to run away from his family.

Juan was pacing from the sofa to the kitchen door. If he hadn't been so on edge, wondering where Annalise was, he would have been proud of walking between the two spots over and over. She'd been arriving at the house each day by 10:00 a.m. It was now nearly noon.

He whirled so fast when the door opened, he wobbled. Putting his hand toward where he thought the wall was, he found nothing. Annalise's hand steadied him.

"Danki," he said. "I should have paid more attention to where I was." Why couldn't she have seen him walking between the sofa and the door?

It was as if she could read his mind, a disconcerting thought. "Your walking looked *gut* when I came in. It isn't easy to concentrate on everything all the time. One of Evie's teachers used to say that."

"If a four-year-old can learn that, I guess a grown man should be able to."

He heard the rustle of her bonnet as she set it on a peg by the door before she took a step toward him. "Don't take this the wrong way, but kids often learn more quickly."

"Old dogs and new tricks, ain't so?"

Her laugh sent a ripple of warmth along him. He appreciated how she laughed with him and not at him.

"Let's start on a new trick that will change your life," she said. "I've been waiting for the cane Dr. Armstrong ordered for you, but let's go with plan B." She pressed a staff into his right hand.

"What is it?"

"The handle off a broom. It's wider than your cane will be, but it's about the same length. I thought you could begin practicing with it."

Horror strangled him as he shook his head. "I don't want to walk around with a cane."

"You won't be walking too far without it."

"I can get around the house."

"Barely, and how are you going to handle the rest of the world?"

He almost said he'd given up on being able to leave the house without his brother's assistance, but he didn't. Not when he was certain she was being extra tough on him so she could say she'd done as the bishop had requested.

Or maybe he was wrong because she continued, "A cane alerts those who can see to the fact that you can't."

"Not something I want to share with the world."

"You don't have anything to be ashamed of."

"I'm not ashamed!" he fired back, though that wasn't true. He *was* ashamed. Not of being unable to see but of being careless while repairing the tractor. He hadn't realized how fragile the steam compartment must have been. What had he done wrong?

"*Gut* because a white cane says that whoever is holding it has little or no vision."

On occasion, he'd seen someone with a white cane and had made sure he stepped aside so they could pass without a collision. He'd pitied them for being dependent upon a cane. Not once had he reckoned he'd ever be in their shoes.

Annalise handed him the broomstick. Lost in his thoughts, he hadn't realized he'd dropped it.

"I wish there was something else I could use," he said more to himself than to her.

"There are other tools, but a white cane is one everyone recognizes. To go without it is asking for trouble." She pulled out a chair from the kitchen table and sat. "One of Evie's therapists told us a story about a blind woman who went out for a walk without her cane. She came to a street corner and waited for the walk signal to beep so she would know it was safe to cross. The signal never came, and she stood there, waiting and waiting. She didn't dare to step into the street, and nobody realized she was blind, so they went past without offering help."

"What happened?"

"She went home. She later learned that the walk signal was under repair along with the crosswalk. If she'd gone into the street, she could have been injured or killed. Someone might have alerted her if they'd seen her cane."

"There aren't too many walk signals along Shushan Bay."

"There are in Charlottetown. When you go there, you'll need to let people know your cane is guiding you. I can show you a few tricks to use it to its best advantage." The chair scraped the floor as she stood. "Shall we get started?"

"I know better than to say no," he drawled.

Her laugh surprised him. "Having a positive attitude is a *gut* start."

Annalise didn't give him a chance to retort. She told him to hold the top of the stick in his right hand and sweep it to his left and right, always keeping the tip on the floor. He tried to do as she instructed, but rocked on his feet.

"Remember what I told you, Juan," she said. "Let your muscles think for themselves. Otherwise you'll stiffen."

"I'm trying."

"I know you are. Here. Let me show you what I mean." She put her hand on his elbow and moved his hand and the stick toward the center of his body. "Like that. You want it to tell you what's on both sides of you."

"By holding it in the middle?" he managed to ask, though he was overwhelmed by waves of sensation rushing along him from where she touched him.

"Patience," she scolded as if he were Evie's age. "This is where you start."

"And then?"

"Move the stick in both directions." As soon as he

started, she said, "Whoa! It's not a baseball bat. Don't swing it. Sweep the tip along the ground."

"I'm trying," he repeated.

She grasped his elbow, and the sweet warmth flowed along him as it had before. A sweet rose scent enveloped him, urging him to turn to face her, and then...

Then what? She was there to teach him a few basic skills. As soon as he mastered them—or better yet, regained his sight—she'd be back on her farm while he stayed on his side of the field dividing them. It would be as if nothing had happened. *That would be for the best*, he thought but convincing himself was harder than he'd expected.

As soon as he'd attempted a few steps, Annalise turned into a drill sergeant, telling him to walk in one direction and then another. She didn't warn him before he ran into furniture.

"Left foot forward, cane to the right," she counted like a drum major. "Right foot forward, cane to the left. Left foot forward, cane to the right. Let it show you what's in front of you. Oh!"

The last was because he ran full speed into the kitchen table, somehow having missed the chairs. He paused and rubbed his leg which had struck the edge.

Annalise pulled out a chair and urged him to sit. Taking the broomstick, she leaned it against the wall with a wooden thunk he wouldn't have noticed a month ago. She moved around the kitchen before setting a glass in front of him.

"Apple cider," she said. "Always refreshing after a workout."

"It *was* a workout." He took a deep drink, draining the glass, which she'd filled halfway. "I hadn't expected something as simple as crossing a room would be so tough."

"Well, you did cross it a few times." She refilled his glass, then set a second one on the table. "I'm thirsty, too."

"*Ja*, calling out those orders must have been tough."

"Really tough. You've got no idea what a sweat I worked up." Chuckling, she sat. Not beside him, but across from him.

Was she keeping distance between them, or was it the habit of sitting so she could face him? He knew better than to ask.

"I thought I was doing okay until I bumped into the table." He slapped his hand on top of it. "Are you sure it didn't jump in front of me?"

"Very sure." Her voice grew serious. "You're doing well, Juan."

"If you think so. I don't see being able to walk between two rooms any great accomplishment. I want to get outside and to work."

"I know you do." Compassion softened her words. "You didn't walk a kilometer right after you took your first step, ain't so?"

"I don't remember. I was a *boppli*."

"In many ways, Juan, you're a *boppli* now because you're learning everything anew. You've got to train your brain and body as you did then."

"You're asking the impossible."

"What? Are you saying you're too old to learn something new? You know that saying about old dogs and tricks isn't always right."

"Whether it's right or wrong, you're asking me to do something that's out of the question when my head is pounding like horseshoes on a road."

She didn't answer right away. Why? Was she questioning if he was being honest about having a headache? He hadn't lied to her.

You haven't always been completely honest, his conscience taunted him.

He ignored it as he remembered how Boaz complained about his exacting wife, who wouldn't give up on an idea, even after it'd been proved wrong.

"Why didn't you tell me your head was bothering you?" she asked.

"I thought you knew it always bothers me."

"Dr. Armstrong—"

"Said the headaches will fade."

"I'm glad to hear that. Are your burns bothering you, too?"

"Not much. Just my head."

Her voice came closer, and he guessed she was slanting toward him from across the table. "I'm sorry if walking with a cane today made you feel worse."

"I've had enough for today. I want to sit and close my eyes for a few minutes." What did it matter if he sat there with his eyes open or shut? He couldn't see either way.

When Juan didn't add anything else, Annalise must have gotten the hint he wanted to be alone. *That* was a lie. He longed to be outside in the sunshine, tending to his animals and to his fields. No longer dependent upon family and neighbors and friends. He wanted his old life. It had had its downs as well as its ups, but it had been his life. Now his life revolved solely around his unseeing eyes and nothing else.

Chapter Six

"You're doing it wrong." Evie's voice rang out from the other side of the living room the next morning. She must have come into the house while Annalise went to feed the animals.

Lucas usually handled those chores, but he'd woken with the symptoms of a cold. He'd contacted Dr. Armstrong, who suggested Lucas not come to Juan's farm until they were certain it was nothing more serious. Juan getting sick on top of his injury might have dire consequences.

Annalise hadn't said what those dire consequences might be when she passed along Lucas's message, but Juan could guess. The slightest germ might prevent him from seeing again. Why else would the *doktor* have warned his brother to stay away? Were his chances of being able to see again so fragile?

"How do you know?" Juan asked, then wished he hadn't. Evie was a little girl who had never experienced a crisp blue autumn sky or the swirling gray of an oncoming thunderstorm cloud. He shouldn't be scolding her.

The *kind*'s voice remained cheery. "I cans hear, silly!"

"Hear what?" he asked.

"I hears your tapping," Evie replied. "Didn't you hears *Mamm*? No tapping! Sweeping. Likes your broom."

"It's not a broom. Just the broom*stick*."

"It's no *gut* if you uses your broom-cane wrong. Sweep, not tap! Likes *Mamm* tolds you to." Though he couldn't see Evie's face, he could imagine her rolling her eyes. Did a *kind* who couldn't see others know how to roll her eyes?

"I cans learns you to uses it better," she said when he didn't reply.

"Maybe tomorrow."

"No! Today. Don't be a-scared."

Juan sighed. The situation was getting worse. A four-year-old was trying to comfort him. He wasn't afraid to use his makeshift cane.

Was he?

The idea shocked him, but had Evie discerned the truth he didn't want to acknowledge? Was he frightened to get proficient with a cane? He wasn't sure, but knew he was terrified he'd have to depend on one for the rest of his life.

Evie's cane tapped his left shoe, then withdrew as she grasped his hand. "Me shows you how."

"Your *mamm*—"

"She is busy with your sheeps. Me shows you how."

Arguing with Evie was as futile as with Annalise. "All right."

"Sweeps your broom-cane." She tightened her grip on his hand. *"Sweeps."*

"I get it. Sweep the tip on the floor."

"Ja." Releasing his hand, she pressed her fingers against the outside of his left shoe. "Swings it this far."

"I can't see how far you're talking about."

"Me knows that. I can't sees either." He had the feeling

she was wearing one of her *mamm*'s vexed expressions. "Juan, puts your broom-cane here." She tapped his shoe.

"And?" he asked.

"Moves it more than two centimeters past. That's three fingers wide for me. One finger for you. You bigger. I smaller."

"For now."

Puzzlement filtered into her voice. "You gettings smaller?"

"No." He fought not to laugh. "I meant you're going to get bigger."

"*Mamm* tolds me I grows like a weed." She paused for a beat before asking, "How does a weed grows?"

"Fast. Have you helped your *mamm* or your great-*grossmammi* pulling weeds?"

"They pulls. I puts in bucket."

That made sense. How could the *kind* tell a weed from a vegetable? His *mamm* hadn't let her *kinder* into her garden until they could name each plant, whether welcome or unwelcome, in the garden.

"So once you've put them in the bucket, is the weeding done?" he asked.

"No! More weeds grows. More weeds by the next week. Oh…"

He smiled as he imagined her adorable face displaying astonishment. Before he'd lost his sight, he'd been awed each time he saw the little girl. Evie was a miniature of her *mamm*, wearing every emotion on her face. He guessed Annalise would be shocked to hear him say that, because he'd seen her try to mask her reactions when she searched for Boaz because she needed his help with something in their barns or fields. She'd always been relieved to find him, but dismayed he was with Juan instead of under her thumb.

He regretted that thought. Since the accident, he'd discovered Annalise wasn't the termagant Boaz had described. She was a bit bossy, but then he had to admit he wasn't the easiest patient because he let his anger and frustration explode as the tractor had. Each time, she remained kind. She insisted, but didn't order.

Not the woman Boaz had described as harping on the smallest matter and lambasting him for doing anything other than working on the farm.

Juan frowned as he thought of how much time his friend had spent with Juan. Boaz had never offered to do any farmwork. Instead he wanted to talk about how enthralling the sea was and how it called to him.

Evie tugged on the broomstick. "Goes a couple of centimeters past your right foot. One finger past. You shoulds bends over and checks if you don't knows where."

The authority in her voice contrasted with her childish voice, and he was amazed to discover he found the combination charming.

She had him repeat the motion until he felt as if he were doing calisthenics, touching his opposite foot over and over. A teacher he'd had when he was in second grade had included a half hour of physical exercises each day in the middle of the afternoon. Cross-toe touches, as she'd called them, had been part of that routine. He hadn't enjoyed them then, and he liked them less when his head spun whenever he raised it.

Each time he faltered, Evie urged him to continue. "Till you knows where your foots are."

"They're in my boots."

"Ha ha," she replied without humor.

"Glad you laughed. I thought it was funny."

"Not funny!"

"Not a little bit?"

"Not a bit." She tapped the broomstick with her cane. "Keeps practicing. No practicing means no gettings better."

"*Ja*, boss."

As she giggled, he bent to touch the outside of his shoes. A big mistake because his head turned into a balloon that wanted to float off in some random direction. Groping for the nearest chair, he sat. The broomstick fell to the floor, its crash resonating through his pounding skull. He cradled his head against his palms as he waited for the light-headedness to recede.

"Here," Evie said softly. "Drinks this."

His hands shook hard, but he managed—with the *kind*'s help—to wrap his fingers around a glass. He hadn't noticed her going to the sink and filling it, but he mumbled his thanks as he swallowed it in a single gulp. He choked and began coughing, which sent more pain across his head.

When she took the glass, he listened as she walked to the sink and filled it. "Drinks slowly," she ordered when she handed it to him.

"I will." His brows lowered, yanking another line of pain along his forehead. "I didn't hear water splashing out of the glass."

"No splashes."

He tilted the glass and sipped. "It's half-full."

"*Ja*."

"How did you know how much water to put in it? Practice?"

"No. Practice won't helps." She took the glass, emptied it into the sink and put it on the table beside him. Picking up his right hand, she folded down his fingers outside the glass except his index finger. The first knuckle of that finger she draped over the top of the glass, using his other fingers to steady it. "Lots of water." She pushed his finger down into the glass to his second knuckle. "Not so much water." She moved his finger down into the glass until the joint connecting it to his hand leaned on the rim. "Littles of water."

"But…"

She didn't let him finish. When she snatched away the glass without warning, he yelped, surprised.

"Komm mol." She pushed the broomstick into his right hand.

He swallowed another gasp when the wood struck his knuckles. If he didn't know better, he'd believe she was giving them a rap because he'd failed to learn the lesson she'd been trying to teach him.

He leaned the stick on his chair. Using the table to guide him, he followed her to the sink where she repeated what she'd said before, but this time having him hold the glass under the tap. He understood what he hadn't before. He let the water fill the glass until it reached his fingertip. Depending which knuckle he used, he could determine how much water went into the glass. It was so simple. No wonder Evie had been frustrated with him.

Taking the glass to where he'd been sitting, his fingers sliding along the table's edge, he left it on the top. He sat again. He was grinning like a fool at being able to accomplish the tasks he once would have done without a second thought.

"Danki, Evie, for teaching me your special way to fill a glass," he said.

"Helping others helps us."

"Did your *mamm* teach you that?"

"Grossmammi Fern says that alls the time."

"Your great-*grossmammi* is a smart woman."

"*Mamm* says *that* alls the time."

He chuckled, and this time the little girl joined in. She was a delightful *kind*. Why, he had to wonder, had Boaz spent so much time with Juan instead of his little girl? His friend had seldom spoken of Evie. Juan couldn't recall a single time Boaz had shared a funny anecdote about his daughter. Why hadn't Juan realized that before?

Disconcerted, Juan wanted to escape the uncomfortable thoughts. "May I see your cane, Evie?"

"Careful. It's ex-cep-tion-al." She spoke as if testing each syllable.

"Is it?" he asked, astonished she knew such a big word.

"*Ja. Mamm* tolds me when I gots it that it's ex-cep-tion-al. Knows why? It takes me where I wants to go. I don't runs into anything. Never."

"I've always run into things, even when I could see."

Evie's voice was laced with sadness. "Maybe you needs a cane before."

"Maybe I did."

She was right to be happy with her hard-won skills. When he'd seen her on a church Sunday, he'd pitied her. What a *dummkopf* he'd been! She was as self-reliant as any other four-year-old. Far more self-reliant than he was.

She placed the cane across his lap. She remained silent as he ran his fingers along it. He hadn't noticed it had sections so it could be folded when not in use. There was also a suppleness to it he hadn't expected.

For the first time, he couldn't wait to get a cane. Dr. Armstrong had offered to get him one right after the accident, but Juan had said no. He'd been too hasty. Too shortsighted, he corrected with a silent, ironic laugh. He'd been so certain his sight would return within hours. Or so afraid that it wouldn't if he admitted he needed help.

Betrayal ripped through him at the thought. Was he giving up hope? He couldn't remember the last time he'd begged God to restore his vision. Maybe those who said God helped people who helped themselves had it right. He should have been grateful that the *doctor* had insisted on ordering him a cane anyhow.

"Ex-cep-tion-al, ain't so?" asked Evie.

Grateful to be freed from the downward spiral of his thoughts, he forced lightness into his voice. "It is ex-cep-tion-al. Don't let Susie chew on it, thinking it's a long bone."

She giggled. "Susie is smart. She knows better. A bone is a bone. My cane is my cane."

"I can't argue with that."

She sounded baffled. "Why woulds you argue about something that is?"

He didn't have an answer. Was that what he'd been doing? Arguing with what couldn't change. Filling a glass wasn't the only lesson Evie had taught him today.

The pattern of Annalise's days flowed one into the next. Doing chores, helping *Grossmammi* Fern with the housework and preparing meals, taking Evie and Susie to Juan's house where she cleaned his house and fed his chickens and goats and sheep and then him.

The difference was that in the past two to three days, Juan was steadier when he stood. His face didn't turn a pasty gray-green, so she guessed his nausea and spinning head had eased.

So today she planned to start the next portion of

the lessons he needed to become more independent. Though she prayed each night and every morning and before and after every meal that he'd regain his vision, she must prepare him in case it didn't.

Today she was going to take him outside.

When she told Juan that, his grin was as big as Evie's when she had an extra cookie. Annalise suspected getting out of the house would be a real treat for Juan.

"Where's Evie?" he asked.

Struggling to keep her shock out of her voice, because she hadn't expected him to ask about her daughter, she said, "She's outside."

"Is that safe with the debris around?"

"Susie is with her." She tried to keep the pride out of her voice and failed.

"She's got Susie on a leash?"

She shook her head, then remembered he couldn't see the motion. "That's not necessary. Evie puts her hand on Susie's head, and they walk around together."

"I thought you said Saint Bernards couldn't be trained as guide dogs."

"I said I'd never heard of one. Maybe Susie is the exception to the rule. She acts as if she understands Evie can't see."

"What if she gets it in her head to take off after a hare or a fox?"

"Evie?"

"Susie!"

Annalise didn't chuckle at his exasperation, though she wanted to. Was Juan always so literal? "I knew what you meant, and I don't know if Susie will stay around or run away as she must have from someone else. That's why I'm not letting them go any farther than your farm or mine. I need to let Evie explore the world like any normal *kind*."

"She's not—" He halted. "I shouldn't have said that."

"You stopped yourself."

"I shouldn't have started."

She sat on the chair facing him. "I understand, Juan. For you, being unable to see is about as far from normal as you can imagine. It's different for Evie. She's never known any other life."

"Doesn't that make you sad?"

"It used to," she admitted, startled she was being so honest with him. "I was devastated when the *doktor* told me she was blind."

He flinched at the word she'd never heard him speak, but she'd learned long ago that avoiding the word didn't help her avoid the truth.

"But?" he asked, and she knew she'd paused too long.

"I learned Evie has ways of perceiving the world I don't. It's possible I could if I tried hard enough, but learning would be difficult."

"As difficult as me learning how to function without my vision?"

"Probably." Squaring her shoulders, she asked, "How are you doing with your temporary cane?"

His smile was grim. "According to Evie, I need a lot more practice."

"She had to struggle to learn, but she did. She can't figure out why you aren't working as hard as she did."

His smile vanished, and she wished she'd considered her words more carefully. How could she when Juan took umbrage at everything she said?

"I'm doing my best, Annalise."

She put her hand over his on the broomstick. "I know

you are. I'm sorry. I shouldn't have said that." Standing, she said, "Let's get you outside."

His shoulders eased from beneath the weight of his tension. "That sounds like an ex-cep-tion-al idea."

"Why are you saying *exceptional* like that?"

"Something I learned from Evie. She's a remarkable kid."

"I think so." She didn't give him a chance to say anything else as she asked him to get up. Having Evie become closer to Juan was something she wasn't sure about. On one hand, a friendship could help Evie and Juan as they faced the ongoing challenges in their lives. What would happen if Juan was able to see once more? Would he push her daughter and her aside, treating them coldly as he had before?

To banish her uneasy thoughts, she centered her attention on helping Juan out of the house. "Step forward. It's time to widen your world."

"I agree. Which foot should I start with?"

"Whichever feels comfortable. If you start with your right, swing the cane to the left."

"Like this?"

She guided his hand to move the stick a bit more in front of him and beyond his feet. "That should be the farthest you swing the cane to the side. Otherwise, you'll be contacting things that aren't in your path."

"Evie showed me, but I'm having a tough time judging how far to go."

"Relax, Juan, and let your muscles do the work. *They* know what to do."

"Easier said than done," he grumbled.

"Relax."

"How can I do that when you're touching me?"

Abruptly she was aware how close they stood. She'd

been focused on helping him, but couldn't ignore his fresh, masculine scent and the warmth of the skin along his hand. Soft hairs brushed her palm, each one a unique caress as he rocked the cane. When his other hand settled atop hers, she knew she should step away. She wasn't in any hurry to get remarried.

Remarried? Where had *that* thought come from? She needed to shake it out of her head and focus on the work Rodney had asked her to do.

As Juan turned to face her, she discovered from his unguarded expression she wasn't the only one no longer intent on his exercises. She repeated her order for him to begin walking with the cane toward the front door.

As he walked away, she shivered. She'd already made a big mistake when she fell in love with Boaz. He'd left her with a broken heart and shattered dreams long before he'd died. She wouldn't risk that again.

Chapter Seven

The front porch was a wondrous place. Juan tilted his face toward the warm sunshine, savoring it. What once had been so commonplace seemed special, something he should never take for granted. Since Annalise had first guided him out the front door two days ago, he'd returned to the porch as soon as he was dressed. He sat on a battered wicker chair and listened to the world awaken.

He was anxious to do more. He could hear work in the nearby fields, including his own. His animals called to one another, sounding content. He wasn't. He wanted to check his crops and tend his livestock. What he could pick up with his ears told him part of the story because he couldn't visualize where his goats were in their pen, whether the chickens were in the grass or on the road in front of the cow barn, or if a squirrel was on the lawn.

From the red dirt lane to the farm, he heard sounds. He held his breath, trying to hear what they were, then smiled because he recognized the assertive footsteps and the sound of wheels with ease. Two of his favorite cousins! Mattie Kuhns and her teenage sister, Daisy Albrecht, had made the families' move to Prince Edward

Island possible. If they'd failed to get the Celtic Knoll farm stand open last year, earning money until his farm and Lucas's farm and their cousin Mark's farm could bring in their first harvests, they would have had to return to Ontario and admit they couldn't build lives for themselves on the Island.

Juan stood and called a greeting. "Mattie! Daisy! How did you get away from the store at this hour?" Using his cane, he went to the top of the porch steps and realized there was a problem. He wasn't certain how to go down them, and Daisy couldn't get her wheelchair up them.

When he'd moved to the farm three months ago, he'd told himself that one of his first priorities had to be building a ramp so Daisy could roll into the house. Somehow, he always found an excuse to postpone the task. If he'd finished it, Daisy could have come up it to sit with him, and he could have gotten off the porch.

Too many "if onlys" taunted him while he sat on the top step which would bring him almost level with his younger cousin in her wheelchair.

"It's easy to get away when you're the boss," Mattie said with a chuckle as the two reached the house.

"Don't let her fool you," Daisy said. "It isn't easy, but she left Daryn in charge with a long—really long—list of instructions."

Their cousin Daryn Yutzy lived with his brother Mark and Mark's wife, Kirsten, in a farm that abutted Lucas's. The teenager had grown more dependable in recent months, eager to earn money to move west and work on a ranch.

Mattie surprised him by giving him a kiss on the cheek as she sat beside him on the top step. "I'm sorry I haven't been over to visit you more."

"Annalise told me you've brought food, and Benjamin's worked in the fields."

"I don't know if that's a *gut* thing or not. Benjamin's never been much of a farmer." He could hear her indulgent smile. Mattie had met and married Benjamin soon after the cousins had come to the Island. Before his accident, Juan had heard rumors that Mattie might be pregnant. He hadn't asked, and she hadn't said anything. Not that she would. A plain woman kept those happy tidings unspoken until her widening waist made the upcoming arrival obvious. "I hear you're going to Charlottetown for more testing."

"Ja." He shook his head. "Dr. Armstrong thinks their more advanced machines might be able to find something to explain why I can't see."

"You don't think they will?"

"I don't want to be disappointed again."

Daisy said, "'But they that wait upon the Lord shall renew their strength; they shall mount up with wings as eagles; they shall run, and not be weary; and they shall walk, and not faint.' That's what it says in Isaiah 40:31." She giggled. "And on the sampler I made for Mattie for her birthday."

"A *wunderbaar* sampler it is, too." Mattie shifted away from him, and he guessed she'd given Daisy a hug when her sister asked for one for her doll. The two sisters had always been close. "Juan, you're looking much better than the last time I saw you."

"Better? Last time you were here, I could see."

There was a pause, then she said, "It was the day after the accident. You were asleep. Lucas let me have a peek so I could see you were all right."

He wasn't sure which comment to react to first. Lucas had put him on display like a circus exhibit?

Why would his brother do that? Mattie hadn't seen anything wrong with it?

Stop it! If someone else in the family had been injured, he would have been among the first to visit in order to find out what had occurred and what he could do to help.

"I'm glad you're here," he said to apologize for his unspoken thoughts. Mattie was perceptive, and she might have guessed what he was thinking. "It'll be *gut* training for Daryn to be in charge for an hour or two."

"That's what Boppi Lynn and I told Mattie," Daisy said.

Juan smiled. Boppi Lynn, a battered doll that Daisy treated like a real *boppli*, was his cousin's constant companion. It often "said" things on behalf of Daisy. They'd learned to go along with Daisy, who had Down syndrome as well as being left paralyzed when she was eight.

His smile wavered. He didn't want people treating him differently because of his accident. He was a grown man, not a *kind* to be indulged.

"Daisy knows as much about running the shop," Mattie added, "as I do. Maybe more. She oversees where the groceries are displayed."

"We're a team." Daisy chuckled. "Boppi Lynn brought you her favorite cookies." Daisy's wheelchair moved, and he drew his feet closer to himself. Dismay sifted into her voice. "I'm not going to run you over, Juan."

"I know," he said to calm her. "I'm sorry."

She wasn't ready to accept his apology. "I haven't hit anyone since I was ten."

"I know. I know. I'm sorry." He couldn't push his frustration onto his cousin. Daisy had accepted her limitations.

She hadn't whined…as he did.

She hadn't been angry with the world…as he was.

She hadn't been furious with God…as he was.

What kind of man couldn't accept God's will when a little girl had?

"Juan said he was sorry, Daisy." Mattie's voice was gentle. "It's as important to be able to accept apologies as to give them, ain't so?"

"Ja," she replied. As if a switch was flipped, her words lightened. "Look! It's Annalise! *Gute mariye,* Annalise!"

His neighbor called a cheerful greeting. "Isn't it a *wunderbaar* morning? We deserve a lot of these after the hard winter we had."

"Lots and lots of them," Daisy agreed.

"Can I take that dish inside for you?" Mattie asked, standing.

"Danki."

Juan caught aromas of garlic and tomato sauce. He hoped it was Annalise's pizza casserole. She'd made it the second day she'd come to help him, and it'd been delicious. He'd considered asking her to make it again, but he didn't want to impose.

As if he'd asked the question aloud, Mattie said, "This smells like your amazing pizza casserole, Annalise. Benjamin hasn't stopped talking about it since you brought it to that potluck for the school."

"I can give you the recipe if you'd like," Annalise said. "It's easy to make, so you can bake it for your husband anytime he'd like."

"Every night would be his choice." Mattie laughed before she edged toward the door. "I'll put the dish on the table so it's ready when you are, Juan."

The door had closed behind her when Daisy asked,

"Juan, aren't you going to try one of Boppi Lynn's cookies? Here."

He assumed she was holding out a plate to him, but how would he select a cookie and not knock the others to the ground? Without a word, Annalise grasped his wrist. She drew his arm forward. When a cookie was placed in his hand, he thanked Daisy.

Annalise said, "Now one for me. These look *wunderbaar*, Daisy." She paused, trying the cookie, he assumed before saying, "They are."

"I agree. Delicious," he said after taking a bite, though he wasn't fond of chocolate chip cookies. More than once, his cousins had teased him for not liking their favorite.

"Really?" asked Annalise as Mattie came out on the porch. "Did the doctor tell you that a side effect of being blown off your feet would be a sudden appreciation for chocolate?"

She was giving him with her jesting question the chance to lighten the tension. He grasped on to it as hard as he held the broomstick.

"Dr. Armstrong said," he drawled as if he didn't have a single care in the world, "that in his professional opinion, he can't be sure what the lasting effects will be. Who knows? Maybe one of them will be that I'll crave chocolate as much as Mattie and Daisy do."

"Impossible," Daisy stated with certainty. "Nobody likes chocolate more than me and Boppi Lynn."

Laughter surrounded him, and he relaxed on the step. Daisy offered her sister a cookie as well as Evie. He hadn't noticed the *kind* arriving with her *mamm*. Something furry slid under his hand. Patting Susie's head, he listened to the conversation. It amazed him how he could guess when someone was about to make a funny comment by how their voice changed. Was that because of a grin? He'd have to ask Annalise to help him confirm his suspicions.

His hand paused in the middle of scratching Susie's ear as he listened to the women talking. Daisy and Evie had left to visit the goats.

"I could sell your woodworking projects in the shop," Mattie said. "If you have any to spare. You'd get a wider audience at the farm shop."

Curiosity taunted him. What sort of things did Annalise create? He remembered Boaz commenting on how much time she wasted in her shed. *Ja, wasted* was the word his friend had used, something that bothered him now. He hadn't given Boaz's complaint much attention because his friend was always grousing over one thing or another, but he had to wonder why he'd found fault with his wife for enjoying a hobby while working beside Juan on the tractor.

Because Boaz was selfish. The thought stunned him. He never would have described his friend that way, but looking through his memories of their times together, Juan had to admit it was true. Boaz had wanted his family's attention on him at the same time he gave so little of his to them.

"I don't know," Annalise was saying.

"Don't know if you want to sell them at the farm shop," Mattie persisted, "or don't know if you'll have enough time this summer?"

He could almost feel both women staring at him. Was he being as selfish as Boaz had been, accepting Annalise's help without considering how much time she was devoting to him? Time she could have spent making whatever she and Mattie were talking about, or with her daughter or *Grossmammi* Fern. He'd noticed when she'd come to collect the pug before the explosion how harried she was.

As the women's conversation moved to Annalise's crafts, he wondered if he would have been as patient and generous with his time as she was. The answer was simple. No. Proof of that? He hadn't built a ramp for his cousin.

I get it, God. I've been selfish. Is that the lesson You have been waiting for me to learn?

Instead of getting an answer to his plaintive question, he was bumped by Susie's head. She butted him with a silent request—or was it an order?—to keep petting her.

Or maybe, he thought, she was reminding him to think more about the needs and wants of those around him.

It was a sobering thought.

Annalise yawned as she followed Evie upstairs that evening. Her daughter was a ball of energy, bouncing on each step. Evie had to be cautious on unfamiliar stairs, measuring them with the tip of her cane for width and depth and height, but she'd gone up and down the staircase in their home so many times, she no longer used her cane. Once Annalise had heard her cane sliding down the steps and had come running, fearing that Evie had fallen. Instead her daughter had been jumping down each step. She hadn't known whether she wanted to scold Evie or congratulate her.

As for Annalise, she could have curled up right in the middle of the staircase and fallen to sleep. It'd been a long day, but a *gut* one.

Despite Juan's many questions after his cousins had left, he'd made progress with the steps. She'd assured him it would be easier once the broomstick was replaced with a cane.

"No, no," Evie said, wagging her finger over the banister. "You can't comes."

Susie and Mei-Mei gazed woefully at her. The dogs weren't friends, but banded together when they wanted to stay overnight in Evie's room.

"You heard her," Annalise said in a stern tone.

The dogs glanced at each other, then their ears perked up. As if on cue, they headed into the kitchen. She guessed *Grossmammi* Fern was there. The dogs knew the elderly woman was likely to sneak them a treat.

Upstairs needed work. The faded wallpaper was coming loose from the walls. Six doors opened off the center hall. Five bedrooms and a bath. The right-hand door at the far end was their destination. Annalise slept across the hall. The middle two rooms were used for storage with *Grossmammi* Fern's bedroom closest to the stairs. The room across from it had become their sewing room, something *Grossmammi* Fern used more often than Annalise did. The door was closed to keep the dogs out. Evie had learned, after stepping on a pin, to go in only with her *mamm* or *Grossmammi* Fern.

Evie led the way into her room. Her small bed was set opposite the window bench where toys and braille books were stored. Clothing hung from pegs along the wall or in the small dresser. The quilt on her bed had been made by Annalise's *mamm* in bright shades of green, blue and pink. Beside it on the floor was a rag rug twisted together from strips of clothing Evie had worn as a *boppli*. Two wooden pieces, one a red horse and the other a small sailing ship, were set on top of the dresser. Annalise had cut and painted each one in her shop while waiting for Evie to be born.

Sitting on the window bench, Annalise gazed out the window as her daughter put on her nightgown. Lamps on a boat glowed from the river across the road. Farther away was the light from Juan's house. She wondered if he was like Evie, who preferred to have lights on when she was in a room. The little girl couldn't explain why.

Justs because, was her answer.

Annalise brushed her daughter's fine hair and plaited it, knowing it would escape by morning and be a halo around her face. She remained in the room while Evie went to brush her teeth. A few weeks ago, her daughter had announced she was old enough to be in the bathroom alone, and Annalise tried to respect the request.

"I'm grateful, God," she murmured, "I have Evie and *Grossmammi* Fern and the two dogs. I wouldn't want to be alone like…"

She glanced at Juan's house. It was empty except for him. How lonely that must be! No wonder he'd been pleased to have Boaz spend time with him. She hadn't thought about that before, and guilt pinched her. She shouldn't have shifted her vexation with her husband onto his friend. That hadn't been right.

"Alls clean, *Mamm*," crowed Evie as she came into the room with a big smile. "Tucks me in?"

"Always, *liebling*." Rising, she went over to the bed. She waited while the little girl climbed in, then drew up the covers before sitting on the bottom of the bed.

"Story?"

"How about a song instead?"

Evie's face screwed up in a perplexed expression. "Song?"

"*Ja*. You'll like this one."

"Okays." She didn't sound certain.

Annalise took a steadying breath and reviewed the lyrics in her head. Satisfied that she remembered them, she began to sing. It was a simple song, one meant to entertain a *kind* and for a *kind* to sing. The tale of a kitten that tried to catch the moon, believing it was in a puddle, was sweet and funny at the same time.

As Annalise finished the chorus and was about to start on the second verse, Evie chirped, "I knows that song."

"*Ja*, you do, Jolly-Jelly-Evie-Belly. Your *daed* used to sing it to you when he tucked you in." She kept her voice light, not wanting to recall how Boaz often was gone by the time Annalise returned downstairs after giving Evie a *gut nacht* kiss. Then he'd started leaving right after supper, always with a promise that he'd be back. Some nights, he didn't keep that promise, staying overnight with a friend or wandering along the river or the bay, lost in his private hopes for the future.

"I likes that song."

"I'll have to ask *Grossmammi* Fern to teach us more of the words. I know three verses. There are a bunch more."

"No."

"No? Why not?"

"Too bigs for lulla—lulla—"

"Lullabies?"

"*Ja*. I'm a bigs girl. No more lullabies."

Though Annalise wished her daughter would reconsider, she said, "It's bedtime, big girl. We've got lots to do tomorrow before we head over to Juan's house."

"I likes Juan," Evie said as she nestled down into the sheets and turned on her side toward Annalise. "You likes him, too, ain't so?"

"Juan is our neighbor, and he's a *gut* one." As she said the words, she knew they were true. She'd been wrong to blame him for Boaz's decisions.

Chapter Eight

Annalise was taking a roast chicken out of the oven late the next afternoon as the van that had transported Juan to the specialists' office in Charlottetown pulled into the front yard. Had the driver made a mistake and brought him to her farm?

She put the roast that was fragrant with rosemary and onions on the stove and tossed the pot holders beside it. She made sure neither dog was lurking in the kitchen, ready to snatch the meat before the humans had the chance to enjoy a single bite. Mei-Mei was in the living room so Annalise shut the door between the two rooms. Outside, the Saint Bernard was ready to greet Juan, as eager as if she hadn't seen him in years.

"Stay, Susie," Annalise said with the calm, quiet tone that worked best with the dog. "You don't want to trip Juan while he's getting out."

Giving her a grumpy expression, Susie obeyed, but her tail swept the grass as her gaze aimed at the van.

Annalise glanced at the thickening clouds on the far side of the river as she went around to the driver's side. From behind the steering wheel, Max Arsenault gave her a large smile, his bushy salt-and-pepper mustache arching across his face.

"Max, I think you took a wrong turn," she said. "Juan's farm is next door."

"He told me to come here," Max replied in his lightly accented English. He'd been born in France before moving to the Island when he was a young man. Rumor said it was because he wanted to marry a woman who lived here, but Annalise wasn't sure if that was true.

"*Ja*, I did," Juan said from the bench behind the driver's seat. "I hoped by stopping here, I could save you from having to bring dinner to my house."

"How will you get home?" She wondered how long it would take them to traverse the field between their farms.

"Lucas will *komm* to take me home in a couple of hours. You told me I needed to get out more, so I'm heeding your advice."

Why this piece of advice and not any of the others? She didn't ask that, not wanting to embarrass him in front of Max.

Annalise stepped aside so Max could get out. He was a large man in every dimension. His shoulders seemed too broad even for the van's doorway, and his stomach pressed over his belt. A bird's nest of dark hair sprouted on his head that reached almost to the roof of the large van.

His beefy hand opened the van's sliding door on the driver's side. The couple of times she and Evie had hired Max to take them to Charlottetown, her daughter had been fascinated by the sliding doors on either side of the van. Annalise had been grateful for the seat belts that kept Evie from testing the windows and door latches during the forty-minute drive to the *doktors'* offices.

Juan edged out. Max kept a hand at the ready in case he started to tumble, but it wasn't necessary. Annalise wondered if Juan even realized Max was there.

He did, because Juan said, "Made it this time, Max. Didn't try to take a nosedive like I did in Charlottetown."

Both men laughed, but Annalise couldn't keep from checking Juan's nose and face to see if they were scraped. She saw no sign of injury. *Lord*, danki *for keeping him safe*.

"We averted trouble, didn't we?" Max gave a full-bellied chuckle.

"We did." Juan reached into the van and took out a folder which he held close to his chest.

Annalise smiled when he also pulled out a white cane with a red band near the bottom. She hoped, like when Evie got her first cane, it would help him. His fingers would grow more sensitive to what he was discerning with its tip, and he'd grow more self-assured.

He began to sweep the cane, bumping it into grass and the uneven ground. "This may be tougher than I thought."

"Put your hand on my shoulder," she said as a breeze teased her skirt, making it dance against her legs, "if that will make it easier for you."

"Danki." His fingers settled on her right shoulder. When she took a single step toward the house, his grip tightened. She bit back a gasp, but he must have realized his fingertips were cutting into her skin, because he loosened his hold. "Sorry."

"It's okay," Annalise replied. Though he didn't know it, helping him today felt important. Not because the bishop asked her to do it but because she owed him an apology for blaming him for Boaz's decisions. She wasn't sure how to say she was sorry for a mistake he hadn't known she'd made.

The van left as they walked to the kitchen door. On each step his fingers brushed her neck, sending cascades of sensation along her. She tried to dampen it, but couldn't. What unsettled her more was that she didn't want to.

When they reached the steps, she asked, "Do you want to climb the steps?"

"What's my other choice?"

"You can sit on the edge of the porch and swing your legs up. Evie does that when she's in a hurry."

He smiled. "Trust Evie to find a *gut* shortcut."

Annalise edged him closer to the porch. When his cane struck the latticework, she lifted his hand off her shoulder and stepped aside as he sat on the edge of the porch. She was startled by how alone she felt when they weren't connected through his fingertips. She didn't want to feel that way about Juan.

She laughed when Susie jumped onto the porch and began to lick Juan's face. She yearned to thank the dog, but instead said, "Susie, give him a chance to stand."

The dog lapped his cheek one more time before moving to meet Annalise at the top of the steps. Patting the dog's head, she couldn't keep from grinning when Juan rubbed his arm against his wet face.

He stood and grimaced. "I used to complain about *Grossmammi* Fern's yappy dog, but at least she didn't try to wash my whole face."

"Because she couldn't reach it."

"Or because she didn't like me."

Walking toward the kitchen door, Annalise said, "Animals are perceptive."

"Ouch!" He grinned. "My goats and chickens like me."

"So you're redeemable."

He laughed, and she was glad to see the stress fall from his shoulders. He hadn't said anything about his visit to the specialists, and she didn't want to press him. It wasn't her business, but she was curious if he'd had similar tests to Evie's.

Making sure she stood far enough away so he wouldn't bump into her—or brush her, bringing forth those quivers racing along her—she said, "There's one step into the kitchen."

He tapped the edge of the threshold with his cane before going in.

"You're doing well with the cane," she said.

"I'm trying to think less about what I'm doing so my muscles can do what's natural for them."

"It's not easy to let go."

He shook his head as he placed the folder on the table. "Far more difficult than I would have guessed."

"How did you fare with the hospital corridors in Charlottetown?"

"They had a wheelchair waiting for me and wheeled me right in for testing. When I was done, they pushed me out to the van. I didn't get a real chance to test-drive my cane."

"It's just as well. As you saw out in the yard, walking on grass and gravel is a lot different from smooth floors." He started to add more, but halted when the door opened and Evie came in with *Grossmammi* Fern and Mei-Mei on her heels.

If the older woman was shocked to see Juan in the kitchen, she showed no sign as she greeted him with almost as much exuberance as Evie. Oddly, the cane Juan carried, something that had frightened other small animals, reassured the pug he wasn't a threat. Maybe because Mei-Mei was accustomed to Evie's and *Grossmammi* Fern's canes and considered them normal. She sniffed it and didn't step aside when he moved. *Grossmammi* Fern caught Juan before he could take a tumble. As he steadied himself, Mei-Mei rushed under the table, hoping someone would drop a piece of chicken.

"Sits by me," Evie said as she grasped Juan's hand. "Shows me your cane."

Consternation stole his smile, and Annalise hurried to say, "Do that while I fix supper. *Danki* for staying here and saving me from having to deliver it to you."

"That makes sense." Fatigue weighed his words, and she guessed his day of testing and waiting for results and then doing it again had been exhausting.

"Shows me your cane," Evie repeated. "Please."

Annalise turned to the counter as the others gathered around her table. She glanced over her shoulder. Evie and Juan sat together on the bench. Did they both want to avoid Boaz's chair, which had been empty since his death?

"Juan is her friend, which is why she wants to sit beside him," *Grossmammi* Fern said as she took out the pan to make gravy. "He's not her *daed.*"

She nodded, not sure how to answer when her thoughts must have been so transparent. *Grossmammi* Fern had been a witness to the disintegration of her grandson's and Annalise's marriage. Did the older woman know how hard Annalise had tried to save it, or did she think, as Boaz had, that if Annalise hadn't been so insistent about him staying home in the evenings with his family, everything would have been fine?

"She knows the difference," *Grossmammi* Fern went on. "As you do."

Annalise was shocked. She blinked back tears as

she put the roast chicken on a cutting board and began to slice it. The older woman usually showed a compassionate heart, but *Grossmammi* Fern's words felt accusatory and hurtful. Or was Boaz's *grossmammi* trying to remind her, while another man sat at their table, that she must keep her late husband in her heart?

That was easier said than done. The Boaz she'd met and fallen in love with remained in her heart, but the man who'd always found an excuse to be somewhere else had never found a place there.

Annalise swallowed the unshed tears, as she'd done so many others, and finished putting the fragrant chicken on a platter. She carried it and a bowl of the gravy *Grossmammi* Fern had made to the table where Evie was giving Juan a long-winded lecture on how to take care of his cane.

"No bangings it into things on purpose," the little girl said.

"I won't." Juan's voice was somber, but his lips were twitching as he tried not to grin.

Going to collect the potatoes, baked corn and green beans, Annalise followed *Grossmammi* Fern, who held chowchow in one hand and a plate with warm rolls and butter in the other. The food was set in the middle of the table, and they sat facing their guest and Evie.

Annalise realized she'd created a problem. Since he'd been blinded, she'd prepared Juan's plate, so he didn't spill food while trying to cut his meat. She wasn't sure how to broach the subject without embarrassing everyone at the table.

Grossmammi Fern asked, "Would you lead us in silent grace, Juan?"

Annalise looked quickly at the older woman, then wondered why she was surprised. In a household of women, *Grossmammi* Fern had been in charge of grace as the eldest, but having a man at their table meant he should set the time for their unspoken prayers.

"Danki," he said. "Let us bow our heads."

They did, but Annalise looked through her lashes to see Evie grasp Juan's hand as her lips moved with her prayers. His fingers closed over hers, holding them. What would happen when Juan no longer needed their help? Would he cut Evie off as her *daed* had?

She barely got in a *Lord,* danki *for the food on our table* before Juan cleared his throat, signaling grace was finished. Glad nobody had been privy to her thoughts, she raised her head.

The problem of Juan serving himself hadn't gone away. Taking a deep breath, she said, *"Grossmammi* Fern, if you'll help Evie, I'll serve Juan and me. That way we can be certain everyone gets a fair share."

"A *wunderbaar* idea," Juan replied. "The food smells so *gut* I might put it all on my plate."

"Nots the gravy!" Evie almost leaped off the bench in her vehemence.

"Your *mamm* will make sure you have some." He tapped her on the nose. "At least a little, little, little bit." When Evie protested, he did the most astounding thing. He winked at Annalise.

Taken aback, she sputtered over her words before she realized she would be smart to fill his plate with roast chicken and the other foods on the table. She skipped the green beans because he didn't like them and instead added more baked corn to his plate.

Was she more amazed that a blind man had winked at her or that he'd winked at her at all? Juan wasn't a flirt like his brother.

As she lifted a forkful of potatoes and gravy, *Gross-*

mammi Fern said, "You haven't said a word about your visit to Charlottetown, Juan. How did it go?"

"They tested my brain and found nothing."

Annalise tried to stifle a laugh, but couldn't. When it erupted from her, Juan frowned as if she'd lost her mind. Maybè she had, but how could she *not* laugh?

He must have realized it, too, because a slow smile slipped across his lips. "I should have said, the *doktors* tested my brain and found nothing wrong."

"I'm sorry." Annalise couldn't halt another chuckle. "I shouldn't be laughing."

"Why not? I did when the *doktor* said the same thing to me."

She wasn't sure whether to be annoyed or amused at how he'd turned the tables on her. As she'd spent too much time irritated at him in the past, she went with amused. She was tired of having to judge each thing she said or did when she was with him.

"So they took pictures of your brain and found nothing wrong. By any chance, did they find anything right?" she asked in a calm voice.

His mouth dropped open, then he shook with laughter. Slapping the arm of the bench, he said, "*Gut* one. I deserved that."

"You did."

With a scowl, *Grossmammi* Fern said, "Can the two of you be serious for a moment?"

"Sorry," Juan said at the same time Annalise murmured, "Forgive me."

"Now," the older woman said with quiet dignity, "tell us, Juan, what the results of the tests were."

He put his fork on his plate and folded his arms on the table. "The tests took far longer than I'd guessed they would."

"Tests takes lots of times," commiserated Evie.

Patting the little girl's shoulder, he said, "Lots and lots of time. They were determined to look inside me with every machine they had there. They used plenty of big words in the reports that are in the folder I brought with me. I don't know why they wanted me to have them because they're sending the same reports to Dr. Armstrong."

"What do the reports say?" Annalise asked.

"I had a concussion, but my brain didn't suffer any long-term damage."

"That's *gut*."

"*Ja*, but it doesn't explain why I can't see."

"It also means there's no reason why your vision won't return," *Grossmammi* Fern said. "Jesus told us if we have the faith the size of a mustard seed, we can move mountains."

"The only thing I'd like to move is my chicken coop." He took a bite before adding, "Lucas tells me he's seen paw prints near it. Something is nosing around it, and I don't want them finding a way in."

"Foxes?" Annalise asked.

"Or coyotes," *Grossmammi* Fern suggested. "Or maybe skunks. They like to attack chicken coops, too."

Juan nodded, and Annalise could sense how relieved he was not to have to talk about the results of his tests. A faint smile eased his expressive lips. "Did you know that foxes and skunks are connected on the Island?"

"How?" Annalise asked. "Other than they both like to invade chicken coops."

"An old Islander told me this story one time when I was in Montague picking up supplies. I'd stopped for a cup of *kaffi* at the Lucky Bean Café on Rue Main…"

"On what?" asked Evie.

"Rue Main. It's 'Main Street' in French, and it's the road that runs through the center of the village. Anyhow," he continued without a pause, "I was having a cup of *kaffi* while I waited for my order to be filled at the hardware store. This old Islander was looking for a seat, so I invited him to sit with me. He accepted and chatted my ear off. He told me that around the turn of the last century, fox fur was the height of fashion among *Englischers*. Most especially black fox fur because black foxes are rare. Entrepreneurs started breeding them, and there was a big rush to get into the business. People sold their homes so they had the cash to purchase a breeding pair."

"That seems rash," *Grossmammi* Fern said. "Did it really happen, or was the guy pulling your leg?"

"I thought he might be, but apparently it happened. The lady pulled out a book from a shelf behind the *kaffi* bar, and she showed me the story of the 'black fur rush.'"

"Skunks ares black, too," Evie said. "Blacks and whites. That's whats *Mamm* says."

Annalise's eyes widened. "Is their black fur how foxes and skunks are connected in your story?"

He grinned. "You're already ahead of me. Because the black fox fur was so expensive, people who wanted to look fashionable but couldn't afford a fox coat, were willing to settle for skunk fur. So the investors imported skunks and began raising them for the market."

"Smelly work, ain't so?"

"I assume they de-scented the skunks so the pelts didn't reek. Imagine a lady walking down the street in a skunk coat, and everyone fleeing from around her because of the odor."

Annalise laughed as Evie used her fingers to clamp

her nose closed like with a clothespin. During the rest of the meal until Lucas came to take his brother home, they laughed and pretended everything was as it should have been. Yet, more than once when Juan thought nobody was paying attention to him, his face grew long with dejection and defeat. The sight cut deep into her heart, and she yearned to devise ways to cheer him.

Only one thing would achieve that. Being able to see again.

As each day passed, she wondered if that would happen.

The breeze was soft and flavored with the scents of mud and marsh grasses edging the river on the far side of the road. Juan sat on his front porch at day's end, took a deep breath and imagined the sky changing into a splatter of reds, pinks and purples as the sun sank toward the opposite shore. In the other direction, where the sky had already surrendered to the night, the first stars would be doing their nightly dance, dancing with the moon and the few planets he could have seen without a telescope. The songbirds were rushing to where they would spend the night while owls and bats came out to hunt and claim the fields beneath the darkened skies.

Closer were his animals. Like other daylight birds, the chickens had disappeared into their coop to roost, safe from predators. Lucas, their cousin Mark and Mattie's husband, Benjamin, had packed a hard earthen wall lined with stones around the base of the henhouse. A fox or skunk could get through it, but it would take a lot of difficult digging, something that couldn't be accomplished in a single night. Any incursions would be seen the next day and repaired, keeping the critters away from the chickens.

Would be seen by someone else.

Juan sighed. He hadn't shared with Annalise and her family last night how one after another, the *doktors* had urged him to find a way to accept that he might never see. Their words and their intentions had been kind, but he'd wanted to rail against each of them, telling them that they needed to have faith in his ability to heal.

He didn't, because his flagging faith had splintered more since the accident. First Boaz's death, then the tractor exploding. Was it easier for Evie, who'd never been able to see and didn't know what she'd lost, or did the *kind* have the courage and faith he once had believed was his?

Shoving his palms against the arm of his chair, Juan stood. He took the cane that was leaning on the chair and went to the door. Entering was simpler with practice.

He went to the desk that was set beneath the window on the opposite side of the room. Groping, he found the second drawer down on the left. He yanked it open and reached in to take out a velveteen pouch. He ran his fingers along it and smiled before using his cane to guide him back onto the porch.

Juan sat in his chair and leaned his cane behind him. As he was opening the pouch, he heard Evie climb the steps toward him.

"What are you doing here so late?" he asked. "Does your *mamm* know where you are?"

She leaned an elbow on the arm of his chair. "*Ja.* She forgots something before, so she comes for it. I comes, too."

"You're right here. Where's your *mamm*?"

"Checkings the goats, she tolds me." As if she could see, she reached out and touched the pouch he held. "Whats you gots?"

Drawing out the musical instrument inside it, he held it out so Evie could examine it with her fingers. They flicked over the stainless steel cover plate and the holes along the top.

"It's a harmonica," he explained. "There have been harmonicas for thousands of years."

"A longs time?"

"A very long time. It's been more than two thousand years since Jesus walked the earth. Harmonicas have been around for at least three thousand years before he was born."

"Two and three? That's five, ain't so?"

"Ja." He chuckled. "You're a smart little girl."

"Mamm says I likes numbers because they are something I cans touch." She began to count, tapping a different finger on his arm as she said, "One…two…three… four…five."

He shouldn't be amazed each time Evie revealed what her *mamm* had taught her. Annalise was doing the same for him. Concepts he'd guessed would take a long time to explain to the little girl—or to him— Annalise made simple. There never was any pity or condescension in her voice.

"Cans I touch it?" Evie asked.

"If you're careful. I've had it since I wasn't much older than you."

"So it's old." She didn't make it a question.

Hoping his smile didn't show, then remembering she couldn't see it any better than he could, he said, "Old and precious."

"I'm precious."

"Is that so?"

"*Ja. Grossmammi* Fern says so." She paused before adding, "She says I'm more precious since *Daed* wents to be with God. I don't knows what that means. Do you?"

His breath caught as she spoke of losing Boaz. He didn't hear grief, only puzzlement. How had a little *kind* come to terms with her *daed*'s death when neither he nor Annalise had?

A verse from Mark came into his mind. The tenth chapter, if he recalled. Jesus's words as parents brought their youngsters to be blessed by Him. *Suffer the little children to come unto Me, and forbid them not: for of such is the kingdom of God.*

He wasn't comparing himself to Jesus. Not by a long shot, but he wondered if there was a lesson in that verse for him. Annalise and Evie had done so much to encourage him. Wasn't it time he returned the favor?

Reaching into the bag beside him, he searched until he found the small, plastic harmonica he'd bought for his cousin Daisy. He'd thought she might like learning to play, but she'd turned him down. She'd chided him, telling him the sound would have hurt Boppi Lynn's ears. That meant, he knew she was afraid it would hurt her own.

Would Evie be as disinterested? He was surprised by how strongly he hoped not. He'd come to enjoy the little girl's comments about everything around them and her help as he tried to navigate a world he could no longer see.

"Would you like to try it?" he asked.

"*Ja!*"

"It's in my right hand."

With a skill he wondered if he'd ever master, she

edged around him and took the harmonica from his hand. There was a long moment of silence. He assumed she was examining it until she asked, "What does a harmonica dos?"

He started to laugh, then realized she was serious. As he replayed their conversation in his head, he discovered he hadn't mentioned it was a musical instrument, one of the few plain folks used.

"When you blow on it, you can make music," he said.

"Shows me. Please."

Would her *mamm* approve of him teaching Evie to play the harmonica? He scanned the yard, straining his ears to catch any sound that would tell him where Annalise was. If she did disapprove and came to halt the lesson, he would apologize…as he should for so many other things. As he'd sat with the family yesterday, he'd thought of how often Boaz had left them behind to visit Juan and work on the tractor. Boaz had complained about Annalise and his *grossmammi* asking him to join them for meals when he, as Boaz had asserted at the time, had more important things to do.

What could have been more important than Boaz's family? Nothing should have been. It was a man's place to take care of his family. That had been drilled into him by his *daed*. Not just by words but by actions, for his *daed* had worked hard day after day, year after year, to provide for his wife and *kinder*.

Boaz hadn't because he'd been thinking only of becoming a lobsterman, which would have taken him away from them farther and longer.

"Shows me. Please," Evie repeated, stealing him from his thoughts.

Shaking them off, he said, "Hold the harmonica in your left hand."

"Which one?"

He faltered, unsure how to explain to the *kind*. Hearing footsteps coming toward the porch, he was relieved when Annalise asked if she might join them.

"Of course," he said.

Evie's excitement filled her voice, "Juan learns me to play the harm…the harm…"

"Harmonica," he supplied.

"What fun!" Annalise sat on the top of the steps. Or he guessed she did by the direction of her voice. She set something beside her. "Don't let Susie and me intrude. I'm going to do some mending. I was going to do it earlier, but we wanted to check the goats and the sheep. They're where they're supposed to be." Her tone lightened. "Now."

"Now?" he asked.

"A couple of the sheep slipped out. I'm not sure who's the greatest escape artist. A goat or a sheep. I got the wanderers back into the field and put a temporary fix on the fence where they'd snuck out. I'll show Lucas where it is tomorrow."

Guilt slashed through Juan. The animals were his responsibility. He should have been gathering them instead of sitting on the porch. Would he be able to do anything on the farm other than be a burden?

As if he'd asked that question, Annalise went on, "*Danki*, Juan, for teaching Evie to play. She's learning a new skill that can entertain us, and I only had to clean Susie and me after wandering through the marsh. I didn't have to wash Evie, too." She laughed, and he heard her daughter giggle.

That sound vanished as water sprayed over him. He tucked his harmonica under his arm to protect it. "Is it raining?"

"No." Annalise chuckled. "Susie shook herself. There's a lot of wet fur on a dog her size."

He was about to agree when Evie pleaded with him to teach her to play. As he began from the first step, he imagined what the four of them would look like to any passerby. A man and a woman with a *kind* and a large dog, sitting on the porch and sharing knowledge from one generation to the next at the end of a day's work.

A family.

If only that passerby knew how impossible creating this family would be. He couldn't relinquish the guilt that shadowed him during the day and tainted his dreams at night. The guilt that if he'd said something or done something and stopped Boaz from going on the boat that day, their lives would now have been very, very different.

Chapter Nine

Juan's face closed as he turned to instruct Evie more about the harmonica, and Annalise looked away. Her daughter would have had a difficult time guessing how taut his shoulders were because his voice remained cheerful. Annalise recognized his expression. She'd seen it often since the accident.

His thoughts were filled with despair. He seldom spoke of his true feelings, acting as if they didn't exist.

Just like you do, her conscience reminded her.

She couldn't deny it was easier to ignore her emotions than deal with them. Before she'd married Boaz, she'd displayed her feelings as enthusiastically as Evie did. She'd tried to portray a more mature poise when she became a wife and a *mamm*. Boaz hadn't been comfortable with her expressing her emotions, though he spoke on and on of his dreams of moving to Prince Edward Island.

"*Mamm*, I can'ts gets this," Evie said, bringing her to the present. "My fingers don'ts works."

Juan's smile looked forced, but Annalise said nothing. He was making a real effort to entertain her daughter.

"Pretend it's a hamburger," he urged, "and you're holding it."

"With one hand," Annalise said as she looked from Juan to her daughter. Reaching out, she helped Evie grip the harmonica and raise it toward her mouth.

"Now whats?" the little girl asked.

His grin became more sincere. "Blow. A harmonica is forgiving. You can cover three holes with your mouth and get a decent note."

Evie put the harmonica to her mouth after taking a deep breath. It exploded out in a single blast through the harmonica. The note battered Annalise's ears.

"*Gut* job," Juan said with more patience than she'd guessed he possessed. "Try again, but don't blow so hard."

Annalise sat and watched as he helped Evie learn the basics of playing a harmonica. Seeing her daughter working on something new delighted her.

"We can do more tomorrow," Juan said after about a half hour of Evie trying to grasp everything he was teaching.

"Plays a song for us." Evie put her harmonica on her lap and clapped her hands together in excitement. "Plays something pretty."

Annalise thought he'd demur, but he didn't. He put the harmonica to his lips and began a song. It was "How Great Thou Art." Unlike the slow tempo of the hymns they sang during a service, the song soared with joy and praise.

She clapped when he was finished and was shocked to see a ruddy blush on his cheeks. Before she could think of how to apologize for her applause while letting him know how impressed she was with his talent, Evie announced, "I plays."

When her daughter blew three clear notes on the harmonica, the same three notes that had begun the hymn, Annalise was shocked anew. She applauded again, this time along with Juan. Evie's grin was so broad it threatened to escape her face.

Evie jumped to her feet. "I goes practice. Okays?"

"Go ahead," Annalise said, "but stay in the yard."

"I plays for Susie and the chickens."

"Gut."

Juan cautioned, "The chickens don't like to be outside after dark."

"Play onc song for them and Susie," Annalise said, "then we should head home and see how *Grossmammi* Fern and Mei-Mei are doing."

She leaned against the step and watched as her daughter skipped across the grass. Skipping had been a tough skill for Evie to master. Unable to see the motion, she'd needed a lot of help before she could understand how to do it without tumbling.

Evie and Susie played on the twilight grass as fireflies flitted overhead, the dog chasing the little girl while Evie evaded her. When Susie paused in mid-lope so she didn't barrel into Evie, Annalise wondered how the dog had come to comprehend what Evie could and couldn't do. The dog watched over her daughter as if she were Evie's nanny.

"Evie has a *gut* ear," Juan said.

Annalise realized he had no idea a beguiling scene was playing out right in front of him. Swallowing her sigh before it could betray her, she said, "Evie has always learned quickly."

"Like music?"

"That's a new interest. I've never been able to get her to sing during church services. The only song she's liked was a lullaby that Boaz used to sing to her, but she told me the other night she didn't want me to sing it to her any longer."

"Did she say why?"

"She said she wasn't a *boppli* any longer, and she didn't need a lullaby to help her fall to sleep." She freed her sigh before adding, "To be honest, though, I think it was because the lullaby was something special between her and her *daed*."

"She doesn't talk about Boaz."

"I know, and I've been making an effort to make him part of our conversations. I don't want her to forget him." She picked up another shirt and saw a small hole where a button had once been. "How many buttons have you lost?"

"Too many. Are you doing *my* mending?"

"Ja."

"You don't need to do that."

"I'm glad to. I like keeping busy. It keeps me from thinking about…" She forced a cheery tone in her voice. "There's no sense in having *gut* shirts sitting in the mending basket."

"You're doing so much already. I shouldn't ask you to do this work, too."

"You didn't ask, and I don't mind." The answer was automatic, but she realized she meant it. She finished the button and tossed the shirt into the wicker basket she'd brought with her. "I'm grateful for you opening Evie's heart to this music." She stood, wiping her hands on her apron. "I should get the casserole into the oven so you'll have food this evening."

"I'm not hungry. Stay here and tell me about the sunset."

"They are pretty here with the river capturing the

colors, ain't so?" She wrapped her arms around her legs as she watched her daughter and the big dog drop into the grass. Sweet notes and discordant ones came from Evie's harmonica, and Susie nuzzled her.

He tilted his head as if he could stare at the porch roof above him. "There are so many things I miss. Not being able to see people's faces to gauge what they're thinking is a challenge. Do you want to know what I miss most?"

"Ja."

"Color."

"Which one?"

"All of them. I've been thinking about the oranges in the sunset," he said.

"I like when the sky goes pink along the horizon in almost every direction."

He nodded. "I remember how sad I was when I learned a *gut* friend was completely color blind. Everything he looked at was gray or white or black. No red, no blue, no green, no yellow. I prayed and prayed for God to heal his eyes so he could see those colors. When I mentioned to my friend how sorry I was that my prayers had gone unanswered, do you know what he said to me?"

"No, what?"

"That he was sorry he didn't get skates for his birthday, too."

"Skates? What did they have to do with him being color blind?"

"To him, having skates was more important than worrying about something he'd never had so he couldn't miss. Later, when he was driving his buggy and had to deal with traffic lights, he might have changed his mind, but I doubt it. As he explained it to me, him missing being able to see colors would be like us being envious of a hound dog's nose. We can't want something we've never experienced."

"But you've experienced color."

"That's why I miss it, though I can pull images out of my memories. Your daughter—" His voice broke.

She reached out to clasp his hand before she could think of the reasons not to. "She doesn't miss what she doesn't know."

"She misses Boaz."

"*J-a-a.*" Her voice cracked on the single word.

"Do you?"

"Of course I do," she answered him as she had everyone else.

Having Juan ask that question was different from other concerned neighbors who'd wanted to offer her solace in the months after Boaz's death. The trite response seemed inadequate now. Juan had been Boaz's friend.

She should—

Something moved near the biggest barn. Something? Or was it someone?

Abruptly she realized her hand was still in Juan's. If someone else saw it, they might get the wrong impression.

Or the right one. She wanted her conscience to shut up, but it went right on taunting her. *What's Juan going to think? You used to avoid him. Now you're holding his hand.*

Drawing away her fingers so quickly she almost jerked him out of his chair, she jumped to her feet. She mumbled about having to get home so Evie could get to bed on time. She didn't give him a chance to say as much as a *gut nacht* before she rushed across the yard, collected her daughter and Susie and hurried toward their farm. Only when she reached her property did she risk a glance back.

And saw nothing but shadows. She wasn't sure if that was *gut* or bad.

"Ready?"

Looking up from the cold cereal he'd prepared with only a few splashes of *millich* missing the bowl, Juan asked, "Ready for what, Lucas?"

"It's Sunday. Church Sunday. Are you ready to go?"

He put down his spoon and grimaced when his fingers dropped into a broad puddle of *millich* on the tablecloth. He'd missed mopping up one spot.

"I wasn't planning on going," Juan replied.

"Why not? You missed the last service, and that was understandable. You weren't steady on your feet. You don't need your eyes to pray or to sing or to praise God. *Komm mol*. It'll do you *gut* to get out and be with other people."

"And have them stare at me as if I'm a pitiful creature."

"If you think you're pitiful," replied Lucas in the tone that warned Juan his brother's temper was rising, "do you think Evie Overgard is pitiful, too?"

"Of course not!"

"I didn't think so. If people stare at you, who cares? It's not as if you can see them, ain't so?"

He gasped at the cruel words.

Lucas went on before Juan could devise a response. "I know that sounded brutal, but something's got to snap you out of your self-pity."

"I don't—"

"*Ja*, you do feel sorry for yourself."

"That wasn't what I was going to say." Well, it hadn't been *all* he'd intended to say. "I don't want to attend church when I haven't learned how to get around my barnyard."

"I get that, but I'm not going to let you sit here, Juan, when being around other people will cheer you up."

"That's what would cheer *you* up," Juan replied. "You're never happier than when you're surrounded by lots of people. If you haven't noticed, I prefer a much smaller crowd."

"A crowd of two?"

"What are you talking about?"

"You know."

Juan's brows lowered in a frown he hoped would convince his brother to change the subject. "If I did, I wouldn't have asked."

The chair on the other side of the table squeaked as Lucas leaned against it. Something else to fix once Juan got his sight back. *If* he did. No, he had to believe it would be *when*, not if.

"You and Annalise have spent a lot of time together."

"She's helping me learn to get around. You know that."

"She asked me to bring you to church."

"She did?" Juan asked, wondering why she hadn't mentioned anything to him first.

Then he realized he knew why. She hadn't wanted to give him time to prepare a litany of excuses as he had for other exercises she'd asked him to do.

"Ja," Lucas said. "So let's go."

"I'll have to change into my *mutze*." He put his hands on his lap and grimaced when he felt damp from where he'd dripped *millich* on his pants. If he'd used an extra napkin as Annalise had suggested, he wouldn't have made a mess. "I need to get cleaned up."

"Then do it! You've got five minutes. If you're not ready, I'm dragging you there with whatever you've got on." He chuckled. "Or don't." He walked out, letting the screen door slam in his wake.

Juan stood and grabbed his cane. He didn't doubt his brother's threat. Lucas was determined to get him to the service, and his brother wouldn't wait a second longer than five minutes to do that.

It took Juan every second of that time to get re-dressed so he could step out on the porch in his black coat and trousers. He'd wanted to trade his work boots for his shoes, but hadn't been able to find one of them. He did wear his black wool hat. Putting it on showed him how much he needed a haircut. He'd have to ask his brother for one before the next church service.

When Lucas mentioned the service was at the Lampels', Juan understood why his brother had been so insistent on him going. Lucas had flirted with almost every young plain woman in their community and beyond, except Aveline Lampel. No other woman had a matchmaking *mamm* like Chalonna Lampel. She was a barracuda with one thing on her mind, making sure her three *kinder* were married as soon as possible. Chalonna had been the first plain person Juan had met after arriving in Prince Edward Island. That encounter had been enough to make him think his family had made a huge mistake leaving Ontario. *Obstinate* was the way most people described her, trying to be kind.

Lucas intended to use his brother as a shield, an excuse not to talk to either *mamm* or daughter. Though Aveline, as far as Juan knew, was unlike her *mamm*. Mattie had mentioned several times how kind Aveline was when shopping at the farm shop, helping their neighbors select what they needed and carrying the groceries to their vehicles. A man would have to think twice before asking Aveline to walk out with him. The prospect of having such an overbearing *mamm*-in-law would quell the bravest man.

When they reached the Lampels' farm, Juan didn't give in to his yearning to hide in the buggy until the service was over. Lucas was right. Juan needed to get out and be around more people. Being alone with his thoughts, when they too often revolved around what he'd do if his sight never returned, was a mistake. He needed other voices to drown out those depressing thoughts.

He was greeted warmly, and he began to wonder why he'd wanted to skip this chance to worship with the *Leit*. Many of the men had been to the farm to do chores or work in the fields. Most of the women had sent food over so Annalise didn't have to cook for him every day. They were his friends, his family.

As he entered the barn where benches had been set, he was grateful he was given a seat near the door. He sensed the curious glances coming his way, but that may have been his imagination working overtime.

He sat and listened to the sounds he'd never paid any attention to before. The creak of the benches as each person chose their place. The shuffle of shoes and the rustle of recently pressed clothing. A *boppli*'s cry, quickly hushed. Whispers, too low for him to pick out the words, buzzed around the space like a swarm of bumblebees. The crinkle of cellophane as someone unwrapped a treat for one of the little *kinder*. Muffled voices came from beyond the closed door behind him where the ordained men had gathered to confer and pray before the service began.

The familiar sounds, though he'd never taken much note of them before, were like a giant embrace. A welcome home he hadn't realized how much he needed. He stood and joined in the first hymn, letting the slow voices wash over his wounded soul.

Each step of the service unfolded as it always had, a balm for his pain and grief. He listened to the singing and the preaching with contentment.

That vanished when Cleason Zehr, one of the ministers, began the longer sermon with, "The seventh verse of the thirty-sixth Psalm tells us, 'How excellent is Thy lovingkindness, O God! therefore the children of men put their trust under the shadow of Thy wings.' As David did so many years ago, so must we."

Juan lowered his eyes toward the floor, not wanting anyone to see his expression. His heart rebelled against the words of a Psalm he once had treasured. How could a loving God let him be blinded? Or keep Evie from seeing the beauty of the world's colors?

Anger welled. He tried to ignore it, wanting to recover the peace he'd found at the beginning of the service. It refused to leave his thoughts and his heart.

By the time the service was over and the communal meal had been consumed, Juan was mired deep within his unhappiness. He could hear the youth playing volleyball and the *kinder* running about with their games. Groups of adults gathered in conversation, but he sat alone leaning against a tree. Was this how it was going to be for the rest of his life?

He folded his arms over his chest as he relaxed against the uneven trunk. The odd thought that he could let it grow around him flickered through his head.

"Are you furious at one thing in particular or the whole world?" asked Annalise from in front of him.

"What?" he asked, as drowsy as if he were half-awake. Had he been falling asleep?

"Better."

"What?" he repeated. Was she trying to be confusing?

With a laugh, she sat not far from him. "How long have you been sitting here, glowering at everyone as if they stole your favorite goat?"

"I was thinking."

"About terrible things, according to your expression."

"Just thinking." He didn't want another lecture on how he should keep a positive attitude and a reminder of how her daughter had overcome every obstacle he now faced.

"If I'm interrupting..."

He almost said she was so she'd go away, but he halted himself. He didn't want to think about his miserable future. "You're not."

"Gut."

She didn't add anything else, and as minutes passed, he began to wonder why she'd come over to talk to him when she wasn't saying a word. Was she waiting for him to bring up a topic? The silence wasn't uncomfortable. In fact, it was pleasing. A couple of times, he started to speak, then stopped, letting peace course over him like the warmth from the sunshine.

When she slipped her arm through his, leaning her head on his shoulder, he knew he should be shocked by her boldness. He wasn't. He was delighted she was so close, that she trusted him as he'd never trusted her. As the sweet warmth of her breath and the intoxicating rose-scented perfume of her soap enveloped him, he imagined tilting her mouth under his and tasting her lips.

The thought halted him from giving in to his yearning for her kiss. How could he be having these thoughts about the woman who used to raise her chin in a defiant pose when he warned her she needed to keep that pitiful excuse for a dog off his land? *Pitiful excuse for a dog… Ja*, he used those exact words more than once. Instead of seeing she was doing her best, he'd given in to his preconceived opinions of her.

So many times he'd listened to sermons urging the *Leit* not to judge others and not to withhold forgiveness. If asked, he would have said he lived by those lessons Jesus had taught, but he hadn't. Worse, he'd judged Annalise without determining the truth for himself.

"Annalise," Juan said, breaking the silence between them.

"Ja?"

"I wanted to tell you that—"

"Juan!" came his brother's shout. "Where are you?"

"Over here," he called, turning in the direction of Lucas's voice. Something brushed his nape, and he reached to push it aside. His fingers found nothing. "We're over here."

"We?" Lucas asked as he paused in front of Juan. "There's no one else here."

"Annalise is here." Had her apron or the hem of her dress swept along his neck when she left? Or had her fingertips stroked him? There had been a human connection that had sent a scrumptious warmth through him. Why had she touched him like that and then rushed away? They'd been sitting in plain sight. Anyone could have seen them, but he couldn't imagine someone thinking that the two of them talking after church was out of the ordinary.

Confusion and concern mingled in his brother's voice.

"Annalise left about a half an hour ago. *Grossmammi* Fern was exhausted after the service, so Annalise took her and Evie home."

"I…" Had it been just a dream?

No, it'd been a warning Annalise was becoming too much a part of his life. He couldn't let gratitude for her assistance convince him that the man who knew her best—her husband—had been wrong about her. She offered a flicker of light in his darkness, but he had to remember she was helping him only because of the bishop's request. Would she have otherwise stood aside and done nothing as she had when Boaz asked for her support for his dreams of becoming a lobsterman?

Coming to his feet, he said, "Sorry. I guess I fell asleep and was dreaming."

"About Annalise?"

He wasn't going to give his brother the satisfaction of answering that loaded question. Instead he said, "Let's go. I'm ready to go home."

"Me, too."

Lucas responded so emphatically that Juan frowned. "Why? You like to stay until almost suppertime."

"Not when Chalonna Lampel is on a matchmaking rampage. *Komm mol.* Let's go!"

Juan nodded, glad of the excuse to leave. Yet, as he walked toward Lucas's buggy, he couldn't stop thinking about how he'd dreamed the gentle caress of Annalise's fingertips across his nape.

Chapter Ten

The next three days dragged whenever Annalise was at Juan's farm. He'd become more reticent than usual, not asking about his livestock. Even Evie couldn't bring him out of his doldrums.

She struggled to keep her dismay from slipping into her voice as she helped him relearn how to use his kitchen. It became obvious he had no interest in what she was trying to teach. His answers were terse, and he shrugged off her fingers when she guided his hands.

Only the fact he had an appointment with Dr. Armstrong at week's end kept her from contacting the *doktor*'s office and sharing her concerns that Juan seemed to be falling into a deep depression. It'd been planned that she would drive him to the appointment, and she hoped Juan wouldn't change his mind about that. By Wednesday afternoon, she'd decided she was going to see Dr. Armstrong with him whether Juan wanted her to or not. Someone had to let the *doktor* know what was going on.

When Juan pushed his chair away and stood, Annalise dropped a spoon and it clattered on the floor.

She bent to retrieve it as he said, "I'm not waiting any longer."

"Waiting for what?"

He went on as if she hadn't spoken, "You can *komm* with me, Annalise, or not. It's up to you."

"*Komm* where?"

"My curiosity about what happened with that tractor has been keeping me awake night after night. I can't wait any longer to figure out why it exploded."

For once, she was relieved he couldn't see her expression, because it had to be a mixture of anticipation and trepidation at the thought of him traversing the barnyard. "You'll need your heaviest work boots."

"I thought the debris had been gathered up and stored in the shed."

"Most of it, but you can—" She corrected herself. "I see slivers of metal in the grass when the sun hits them just right. I've picked up and tossed a bunch. I'm sure there are plenty more."

He walked to the closet with an ease he hadn't had a week ago. Getting his boots out, he sat on a nearby bench to pull them on.

She opened the door and stepped aside for him to go out first. "I've told Evie not to go into that area."

"How do you keep her out? She's as headstrong as..."

"As me?" she suggested when his voice trailed off. "I know I can be stubborn, but I won't apologize for doing what is right for my family."

"I'm not asking you to. I'm curious how you convinced Evie to listen to you when she loves to explore every corner of the farm. She's always telling me how the sheep are doing or the chickens or asking me when the potatoes will blossom." His brows lowered. "You do know the little fruits grown by the potato blossoms are poisonous along with the potato plant's leaves, ain't so? You'll want to keep Evie and the dogs out of the fields then."

"Especially Mei-Mei. That dog will eat anything. Even dandelions. It doesn't matter to her whether they're yellow or gone to seed."

"You didn't answer my question about how you keep Evie away from the debris area."

"You didn't give me a chance."

When he chuckled, she had to smile. It was the first time she'd heard anything but cranky words from him since Sunday. Was he becoming more accepting of the different path his life had taken? She doubted that, because he hadn't given up his belief that his eyesight would return.

"I told Evie," she said as they crossed the porch, "to stay away from the area of the explosion in order to protect Susie's paws from any metal in the grass."

"In other words, you manipulated the truth."

"No, that *is* the truth. You and I can wear shoes, but a dog can't. I don't want Susie to get a metal sliver in her paw. So far, the request has worked."

He put his hand on the railing. The hours of practice while she taught him to use his cane to guide him must have become ingrained in his muscles.

She watched, silent, while he used his cane to measure the steps and make sure he had an image of them in his mind before he took his first step. Though he'd been on these steps many times, he'd heeded her instruction never to assume that nothing had changed.

Annalise's fingers began to shake as the two of them crossed the yard in silence. She hadn't been to the site of the explosion since the day she'd found Juan in the mud. Approaching that spot woke the emotions she'd experienced that day.

Shock.

Terror.

Hope that she wasn't too late to save her neighbor.

Comfort in knowing that God would see them through whatever happened next.

She longed for that comfort now when she couldn't figure out why Juan seemed determined to shut himself off from the world. At least, he hadn't lost his curiosity. That must be a *gut* sign he was healing.

Juan said, "It might be better if I hold on to you so you can guide me around anything in my way."

"Ja." She willed her shoulders not to quake beneath his fingers. He had an array of emotions dogging his steps and taunting him, too. "We need to go into your old equipment shed."

"All right." His face was drawn, revealing lines she'd never seen before. It must be taking every ounce of his courage to put one foot in front of the other. Her bravery was being taxed to the point she wanted to spin about and flee to the house.

It's just debris. Even so, she shivered as they went into the shed.

The interior smelled of oil and gas and damp soil. She waited for her eyes to adjust. The space had enough room for a couple of pieces of field equipment. Now only the broken parts of the tractor were stored there.

"Has anyone been here," Juan asked, "since they put the remains of the tractor in here? Or did Lucas just shove the door shut and walk away?"

"I don't know. You'd have to ask your brother." She hesitated, then asked, "Why do you think he just shoved the door shut and left?"

"Haven't you noticed? That's how Lucas lives his life. When something gets too serious or too real, he leaves."

Astonished, she recalled how seldom Juan's brother had gone into the house when he came to the farm to do chores. Since Juan was able to get out to the porch, Lucas had called a greeting before he hurried home to his own farm.

"I hadn't noticed," she admitted. "I guess I didn't pay attention to anything but how *wunderbaar* he's been to do the milking twice a day."

"He has been great to do that." He put his hand on her arm. "Don't think I'm deriding my brother. Lucas is my brother, and I love him. However, I know what he's like. He doesn't want to be around anything that's too weighty. He'd prefer to let someone else solve the tough problems."

"He brought you to services on Sunday."

That had been the wrong thing to say. He released her shoulder and turned away.

What happened on Sunday? she wanted to shout. Instead, she said, "You can move about two-thirds of a meter in any direction. More than that, and you'll run into broken pieces."

He held out his cane to check her advance. Because he'd learned what she'd taught him or because he didn't trust her? What had caused him to revert to the icy neighbor he'd been before the accident?

The cane's tip clanked against a piece of metal, and he leaned forward to touch the top of the pile. He ran his fingers along the rusty debris.

"It's less than I expected," he said.

"There weren't many big pieces left. The explosion blew everything into confetti."

"Rusty, metal confetti?" His laugh was as strained as his voice, and she wondered what thoughts, which memories, what dashed hopes were flooding his mind.

She doubted they were the same as hers. How many times had she begged Boaz to stay at home with her and Evie and *Grossmammi* Fern instead of joining Juan to work on his ancient tractor? How many times had he failed to listen to her, too eager for his friend's company instead of theirs? How long would he have kept coming to Juan's barn if he hadn't drowned?

Juan replied as if she'd asked those questions aloud, "Boaz stopped helping me with this even before I moved onto the farm. About two months before he died."

"He did?" Her voice came out in a squeak.

"Ja." He paused, then asked, "Did he tell you he was coming here?"

She searched her memories, trying to avoid the most painful ones. It was impossible. The last few months of Boaz's life had created little but despair for her.

"He didn't say where he was going," she said as she dug into the memories she preferred to leave alone, the ones that were like a scab on a slowly healing wound. "I assumed he was with you, because it was where he'd always gone in the evenings."

"Earlier, *ja*, but not just before he died."

"He must have been with the crew from the lobster boat." She didn't see any reason to make it a question.

"You're probably right. I guess we both should have questioned what he was up to."

"Would it have made any difference? He wasn't going to stop chasing his latest dream."

When Juan put our his hand, his fingers found her sleeve without hesitation. He was learning, as she'd urged him, to trust his muscles to know the way. "I'm sorry, Annalise."

Her momentary satisfaction at how well he was progressing vanished as he stepped away, his face blank. He hadn't come to terms yet with whatever had upset him on Sunday. If he didn't want her help with that, she must not offer it. Her job was to help him manage living sightless in a sighted world. Nothing more.

"Was there something you wanted to check?" Annalise couldn't keep the sharpness from her voice.

"Do you see a bright red tank? Or what's left of it?"

"Let me look." She edged around the pile of rusted debris. "How big?"

He held his hands over a meter apart. "That would have been the original size."

"No, I don't see anything like that. It's probably in small pieces."

"Do you see any red pieces? The tank was the only part painted red."

Annalise moved to where she'd have another angle of the broken metal. "There's one. No, two."

"Can you get them out without getting hurt?"

"*Ja.* They're on the outer edges of the pile." She took a step closer. "Stay back. I don't know what will fall when I pull them out."

"Be careful."

She nodded, biting her lower lip as she stretched as far as she could to grasp the two pieces of red metal. With a rattle, the red fragments came out. A single scrap tumbled onto her right sneaker, but the rest of the pile stayed in place.

"Got them!" She backed away, keeping a close eye on the stack in case it fell.

"What condition are they in?" Juan asked.

Annalise turned the pieces over and examined them from every side. She almost dropped them when the sharp edge on one drew a bloody line across her thumb. Keeping her wince of pain out of her voice, she said, "Their edges have been pressed outward."

"Let me see."

She bit her lip as she handed him the ruined part. Weeks ago, they would have cringed at the commonplace phrase. Juan spoke now without hesitation, his thoughts focused on the piece of metal.

"Be careful," she said. "The edges are sharp."

His head jerked up. "Did you cut yourself?"

"A small scratch."

"Is it bleeding?"

"A little. Juan, I've been cut worse chopping onions."

"Your kitchen knife is much cleaner than these metal parts that were blown all over the barnyard. Is your tetanus shot up-to-date?"

"I don't know."

His brows lowered. "You work in a woodshop with sharp tools, and you haven't kept track of when you're due for your next tetanus shot?"

"My tools aren't rusty!" She didn't add that she hadn't spent time in her workshop since before his accident.

"Tetanus is caused by puncture wounds, not just by rusty metal."

"I didn't know that."

He held the piece of metal in her direction, something he couldn't have managed last week. "Put it aside. We need to get you a shot."

"I'll be fine."

"You can't know that for sure."

"I've never had any problem."

"Never say never. You need a tetanus shot."

She sighed and looked at her thumb. It was an innocuous injury, but Juan was right. She must make sure it didn't get infected. More important, she might have a chance to talk to Dr. Armstrong about Juan's odd behavior.

"All right," she said, smiling. "Let's take care of what needs to be taken care of."

Juan hadn't imagined he'd come to the *doktor*'s office in Montague a couple of days before his scheduled visit. He was amazed Annalise had agreed with his request. After she'd cleaned and bandaged her thumb, she'd hitched his horse to his buggy. Telling him to get in had been the last words she'd spoken until they reached the *doktor*'s office in Montague.

She went to the receptionist, leaving him to perch on a hard plastic chair. She returned to let him know Dr. Armstrong could fit her into his schedule, though they'd have about a fifteen-minute wait.

People entered and left the reception area, everyone talking in hushed voices. He heard a set of crutches clump toward him, and he pulled in his feet in case they were sticking out too far.

A teenage boy said, "Thanks, man."

The doors to the parking lot and to the examination rooms continued to open and close, but no one else spoke to him.

"How are you doing, Annalise?" he asked.

"I'll be glad when it's over," she said.

"Are you afraid of shots?"

"No," she said, but he heard the tremor in her voice. "I'm not looking forward to having a sore arm."

"Better a sore arm than lockjaw."

"Must you use a cliché?"

"When it says something better than I can, I do."

She shifted on her chair, and he guessed she found them as uncomfortable as he did. "You should have stayed on the farm. I could have handled this."

"I wanted to make sure you didn't change your mind about seeing the *doktor*."

"No, your advice makes sense. I'm sorry I couldn't help you discover more about the pieces of the tractor."

"You did. That the edges were pushed outward shows the explosion came from inside the water tank."

"I thought you'd guessed that."

"I like to have my guesses affirmed." He sighed. "I'd hoped there would be less damage, so the tractor could be put back together."

"Now it's like a million-piece jigsaw puzzle."

Juan was glad when someone called Annalise's name. He rose to go with her and expected her to tell him to stay where he was. She didn't, and he followed her to where a nurse welcomed them. Knowing he was slowing everyone down as he walked along the hallway, he let Annalise guide him into a room and urge him to sit on another chair as uncomfortable as the ones in the waiting room.

While typing on what must have been a computer, the nurse asked a few questions about what had brought them in as well as what had caused the cut to Annalise's thumb. Annalise answered each calmly.

"Good," the nurse said. "Dr. Armstrong will be in as soon as he finishes with another patient."

Silence claimed the room as the nurse left. Not the *wunderbaar* silence from his dream on Sunday afternoon, but a strained silence. How frightened was Annalise of getting a shot? Or was her wound worse than she'd told him and she was in pain?

That she was at the *doktor*'s office was his fault. He could have waited until his brother had visited and gone out to the shed then. Lucas had put him off each time he'd mentioned the debris, saying it could wait. That had irritated Juan, but his brother had been correct to be cautious.

The door opened, and the *doktor* came in, greeting them before saying, "Let's have a look, Annalise." He must have done that because he said, "Not too bad, and you've cleaned it well."

"Juan thought I should get a tetanus shot."

"A good idea." He walked away from Juan's side of the room and opened a cabinet and two different drawers. "Have you had one of these before?"

"*Ja*, and I remember having a sore arm."

"An unfortunate side effect, but it won't last more than a day or two." Another pause, then he said, "There you go."

"*Danki*, Dr. Armstrong."

"You're welcome." He dropped the syringe into the locked refuse container. "I'm glad you came in. I'm sure nothing would have happened, but it's always a good idea to be overcautious."

"That's Juan for you. Like a hen guarding her chicks." Before he could defend himself, she added, "Could I talk to you about something, Dr. Armstrong? In private?"

The *doktor* said, "Juan, do you need help getting to the waiting room?"

"I can do it."

"Glad to hear that."

Curious what Annalise wanted to discuss with the *doktor* without him overhearing, Juan found his way to the waiting room. The hall was straight with no other corridors branching off it, and someone was coming in from the waiting room as he reached the door, so he didn't walk past it.

A few minutes later, Annalise came out. She walked to him and said, "We can go."

"Is everything okay?"

"I'm praying so." She held out her arm, nudging him.

He took it, silencing the rest of his questions. Her terse answer let him know she didn't want to say more. He needed to respect that.

As they went to the buggy, the distant rumble of thunder warned of an approaching storm. What a peculiar situation! He couldn't see lightning, so he had no warning when the next crack would sound.

"How close is the storm?" Juan asked once they were seated side by side in the buggy.

"Let me check." It took almost a minute before he heard more thunder and she added, "About two kilometers."

They wouldn't beat the storm to shelter. The buggy had no windows, so rain would lash them. Reaching behind the seat, he pulled out a tarp he kept there. He told Annalise to drape one end over herself, and he did the same with the other side. It was scanty protection, but it was the best he could offer.

They weren't more than a few meters on their way before the wind tried to pull the tarp off them. Rain followed, each drop a separate arrow trying to pierce their skin. When the buggy slowed, he knew the visibility must have been decreased.

"Should we pull off and wait out the storm?" Juan asked.

"If it gets worse, we'll have to. I don't want to at-

tempt the roundabout when other drivers can't see us."
Her hand slapped down the tarp, trying to keep it from
flying away. "I'm hoping the storm will pass before
we get there."

As they drove up the hill leading away from the Montague River, the wind continued to blow, but the rain
slowed. The storm had gone to the east of their route,
sideswiping them. He took the tarp when Annalise lifted
it off and tossed it in the back. He'd let it dry when he
got home.

No, he'd have to ask her or his brother or someone
else to do that. He doubted he could handle the heavy,
wet fabric and his cane. Hanging it over his porch rail
might be impossible for him as well. He tried to tamp
down his frustration, but it flared through him.

By the time the buggy turned onto Georgetown
Road, the rain had begun to fall again, but more gently.
Annalise said, "We're almost to your place. We're about
to pass those tourist cottages in the corner of the river."

"Let's go there."

"Where?"

"The cottages. Turn onto the road and follow it to the
one farthest down the hill."

"Isn't it private property?"

He smiled, hoping she was looking in his direction.
"I did some painting for the owner when I first came to
the Island, and he told me to feel free to use their beach
whenever I wanted."

"You want to go to the river?"

"Ja."

Disbelief heightened her voice. "Why? It's raining."

"I know."

"You want to go for a walk?"

"Annalise," he said.

"*Ja?*"

She was facing him. *Gut.* Maybe she'd hear his sincerity.

"You don't have to go with me," he said, "but I need fresh air and a taste of something wild. The only places I've been since the accident have been *doktors'* quiet offices and laboratories. Everyone spoke in whispers, and their shoes were silent on the floors."

She didn't say anything, and he wondered if she would drive by the red-dirt road. Then he felt the buggy slow before it took the sharp corner that dipped down from the main road. The wheels bounced on the uneven road and the tree roots that reached out into it. He gripped the buggy's side as the rough ride continued until she slowed them to a stop.

Juan reached for his cane when she jumped out and went to tie up the horse. He eased out and tried to recreate the scene around him from his memory.

There were a handful of small cottages along the road. Across an expanse of green grass, two larger houses were part of the compound. The river ran to his right where a crescent beach curved along a narrow cove.

"All set?" Annalise asked from near his elbow.

Instead of answering, he put his hand on her arm and let her guide him through the wet grass on the gentle slope down to the beach. The previous times he'd been there, he'd seen the bright red sand topped by stones, shells, sea glass and blackened kelp. His boots crunched on the uneven surface as water squeezed up from the sand. He walked to the water's edge, knowing how wide the river was here and wondering if the opposite shore was visible through the rain. Her skirt flapped against his legs as he held his face up so the wind and the rain could wash over it.

He took a deep breath and let the dull thumps of the rain striking the river's surface resonate through his senses. The air tasted of mud and the nearby marsh and salt. Something rustled, and he guessed an animal was slipping through bushes to his right.

That was confirmed when Annalise whispered, "There's a fox on the hunt. I caught sight of its bushy tail."

"The birds have nests in the marsh. The fox is hoping to steal eggs for its supper." He drew in another breath as he said, "This is *wunderbaar*. For the first time in nearly a month, I feel alive."

"Really?"

"I've hated being kept indoors like someone's pampered pet. I'm used to being out in the weather, the *gut* and the bad. Instead of smooth wooden floors beneath my feet, I want the ground, even if it's not as easy to walk on."

"Tomorrow we'll do more work in the yard." She shivered. "If it's not rainy."

"You're getting cold."

"And wet."

"That happens when you don't know enough to get out of the rain."

"Me?" Her voice took on a mock anger. "You're the one who dragged us down to the river in the midst of a storm. Don't tell Evie. She's been asking me to take her to the beach, and I've told her I would sometime."

"When you're done helping me?"

"Before that, I hope." She hesitated, then said, "That will change if your sight returns."

"A lot will change *when* that happens." He emphasized the word as he turned to head to the buggy. He didn't sweep his path with his cane, and on his first step off the beach, his foot caught on a large chunk of driftwood, sending him sprawling in the wet grass.

He grimaced as he sat. Running his hands through the grass, spraying himself with more water, he searched for his cane. Where had it gone?

It was pressed into his right hand as Annalise said, "You've just learned what happens when you don't use your cane." She put her arms around him to help him to stand.

Sensation soared through him like a seagull gliding above the waves, spiraling out from where she touched him. He thought of how he could slant her across his lap while he claimed her lips. He imagined her soft against him, her arms no longer around his waist but draping over his shoulders. If he took her wrist and drew her down—

She moaned. Not with yearning, but with pain. Her arms snapped back from him, and he dropped to the ground with a thud that resonated through his skull.

"Sorry," she said. "My arm cramped from the shot. Let's try again."

He waved her away, not wanting her to hurt her arm. As important, he knew the danger of being too close to her when nobody else was nearby. He couldn't let gratitude for her help in navigating his new life evolve into a different emotion. That would be stupid. If he never regained his sight, she didn't need to be burdened with two blind people in her life. If he could see, he had to focus on catching up with his farm work and wouldn't have time for any sort of relationship other than as neighbors who waved across the field.

"It's okay, Annalise," he replied in a taut tone, annoyed by his thoughts, though he couldn't have said which one bothered him the most. "I'm not a toddler who's going to cry if I tip over. I'm a man who understands the risks I'm taking. You don't need to coddle me."

"I'm not coddling you. I want you to become more independent."

He got up and wiped his wet hands on his wet trousers. "So you can be done babysitting me?"

When she gasped at his harsh words, he wished he could pull them back. His anger shouldn't have been aimed at her.

Her sneakers swished through the grass, moving away. If she got too far ahead, he wouldn't be able to use the sound of her steps to guide him. He could walk in circles on the wide yard, never finding the buggy.

Panic clutched him as he thought of hour after hour of trying to find the place where they'd left the buggy. He hadn't paid enough attention on the way to the beach to retrace the path.

She had every right to abandon him after what he'd said. He wasn't angry with her. He was angry with God who'd left him so helpless and frustrated. All she'd done was try to help, and he'd treated her as if she was less than the dirt under his feet.

Cold sweat trickled down his spine as he strained to hear the horse's movements or the rattle of harness and wheels from the buggy. Nothing. How long would he wander about before someone took pity on him? Pity! *Ach*, how he despised the word! He was pitiful, turning on the one person who had so many reasons not to teach him.

Then a hand took his left one and put it on a slender arm. Annalise didn't say anything as she led him in the opposite direction from where he'd been headed. Words of apology filled his mind, but he didn't speak a single one. The chasm that had reopened between them might have been for the best.

So he kept telling himself.

He wondered how many times he'd have to before he began to believe it.

Chapter Eleven

Annalise arrived with Evie and the Saint Bernard at Juan's farm around midmorning two days later. She would be taking him to see Dr. Armstrong that afternoon. When she found him outside, she wasn't astonished. He'd been so unnerved by getting turned around by the river that he'd been working on his navigational skills in his yard and then along the road between their farms since. He was gaining more confidence, even as he was keeping distance between them.

Or at least it felt like that. If she went into a room, he hurried out. If she stepped onto the porch, he had something to do near the chicken coop. The two-step dance of avoiding her went on the whole time she was on his farm. At first, she'd wanted to believe she was making something out of nothing, but it became obvious he wanted to keep as far from her as he could.

Had he experienced, too, the sudden rush of warmth when she put her arms around him to help him to his feet? It had discomposed her so much that she'd backed away like a skittish cat. She'd used the excuse of an aching arm. Her arm had been sore, but not enough not to help him.

She didn't push the issue of how he was growing reckless with his walks along the road. There weren't a lot of cars, but most were driven by tourists who weren't familiar with the twists along the road or the fact there were slower-moving vehicles and the occasional pedestrian.

Today he wasn't striding along the road. He was resting his arms on the fence around the sheep's field. If she hadn't known he couldn't see the sheep, she would have thought he was assessing each one. She dared to believe—for a second—that maybe he could see at last. As she got closer, she saw the narrow pucker between his brows that matched his frown, and she knew nothing had changed.

"Something wrong with the sheep?" she asked in lieu of a greeting.

He turned his head as Evie and Susie galloped past him, playing a game that defied definition. Annalise tried not to interfere, other than to make sure they didn't run into anyone or anything. When she saw Susie nudge Evie past the chickens wandering around the barnyard, Annalise smiled. The dog somehow knew that her daughter needed more guidance than other *kinder*.

"I need to move the sheep," Juan said. "If they stay much longer in that field, they will crop the grass so close to its roots it won't grow back."

"They do that?" Had he shifted away from her, or was her imagination working overtime?

He nodded. "Unlike cows or goats or horses, sheep have to be taken out of a field before they destroy it. Cows, horses and goats also have to be moved when the greenery runs out, but grass grows well in their wake."

"Where do the sheep have to go?"

He gestured toward the smaller barn. "Behind the

tractor shed. The grass is lush there, and they should be fine there for at least a month, possibly two."

"Then let's move them." She walked to the porch and left her bag and her bonnet there.

Juan was regarding her with bafflement when she returned. "Move them? The two of us?"

"Three of us. Evie will be glad to help."

He shook his head. "I think it'd be wiser to wait for Lucas or someone else to come."

"When will Lucas or someone else be here?"

His mouth tightened. "I don't know."

"We can do it. It can't be more than fifty meters, and there are three of us."

"Two of us can't see."

She refused to back down, though she was beginning to see possible problems. There were spaces between the buildings, and the sheep would take advantage of any opportunity to go where they shouldn't. "You can hear, and the sheep won't be silent as they walk from one field to the other."

"No, they baa as if they're hoping another sheep will welcome them into the new field."

"Well, there you go. You'll be able to hear them, and so will Evie." She looked at the route. "There are two gaps between the fields. One before the flock gets to the big barn and then the space between the two barns. Neither is more than a few meters across. If you stand in one gap and Evie in the other—"

"There are three gaps. The gate to the other field is at least three meters beyond the tractor shed."

"I'll take the first gap, and then get to the third one before the sheep reach it. Meanwhile you can move along with the sheep in case they take it into their heads to bolt."

"All it takes is one, and the others will follow."

"I know. I've had your sheep over on my farm several times. Remember?"

His taut face was her answer. Words of apology seared her tongue. She hadn't meant to be accusatory.

He turned away, and she wondered what he was seeing in his mind. He'd spent enough time on the farm to believe he had every part of it memorized. In the past month, he'd learned that wasn't so.

"Is there a storm coming in?" he asked.

His question took her by surprise. "No. Why do you think that?"

"I keep seeing what looks like lightning from the corners of my eyes."

"Both?"

"*Ja*. Do you think it means something?"

She chose her words carefully. "I don't know. Has this been happening for long?"

"A day or two." He cleared his throat. "After our stop by the river."

"It may be the change I've been praying for."

"You've been praying for me?"

"Why are you asking that? Why wouldn't I pray for your sight to be restored? It's what your heart has been crying out for."

The wrong thing to say, she realized, when he turned toward her. Though his eyes couldn't perceive her, she felt captured by them. She looked away, glad he hadn't seen her strange reaction. A flutter twisted in her middle, shocking her. It reminded her of how she once had reacted when Boaz walked by or stopped and spoke with her.

It couldn't be the same. She'd been attracted to Boaz and delighted when he paid her attention. Her relationship with Juan was different. He didn't make any attempt to persuade her to walk out with him. No pretty words or gushing compliments had come her way. That was his brother's way. Boaz's as well. Her late husband had been more like Lucas than Juan.

Instead of laying on adulation, Juan spoke to her honestly. He didn't sugarcoat anything. It startled her that she knew more about Juan and his opinions and view of life and faith in a month than she'd learned about her husband in the nearly six years of their marriage. She'd told herself that she'd understood how Boaz felt and what he believed, but she'd been wrong. He'd been one man while they were courting and another after they spoke their marriage vows.

"*Danki*, Annalise," he said. "My prayers have been weak, so I doubly appreciate yours."

She blinked back tears. Deeply touched, she managed to say, "Shall we get that flock on its way so we don't smell like sheep when we go to Dr. Armstrong's office?"

When Juan agreed, she guessed he was as eager as she was to change the subject and break the invisible thread connecting them. She called Evie over to them and listened while Juan explained what they needed to do and not do.

"No loud noises," he said. "You can wave your arms at them to get them together, but if you yell, they'll scatter. Talk to them in a normal voice. That won't spook them. Remember they aren't smart, and they'll run over you if you jump out in front of them."

Annalise helped Juan and Evie get into place before she opened the gate. She looked around. Where was the dog? She could have used Susie's help with getting the flock moving. Then she discovered she didn't need the dog. As soon as she opened the gate, the sheep poured through.

Letting the others know that the sheep were coming, she stayed behind them. She'd rush past them and hope they'd keep going in a straight path once she passed the first two gaps. At each, a sheep or two started to bolt, but each time, either Juan's or Evie's waving arms made them change their minds.

As she stepped around them to get to the final gap, she halted in midstep.

Susie was already there. But not the happy-go-lucky dog who ran around the farm. Susie was all business. Sitting with her tongue lolling out of the side of her jowls, she didn't move except for her eyes. They were focused on the sheep. The lead one faltered when it saw her, then hurried on when she remained where she was. The others followed, glancing at the dog watching them. One sheep edged toward the far side of the road.

The dog raised her head. She didn't make a sound, but the sheep got the message and hurried along with the rest of the flock. As the final sheep passed, Susie rose with dignity and walked after them, never barking or snapping.

Annalise hurried to shut the gate behind a straggler who rushed through when Susie took a step closer. Turning, she watched Susie alter from a serious working dog to her usual silly self. She lapped Annalise's hand and gazed up at her as if to ask, *We did a gut job, ain't so?* Patting the dog, she waited for Juan and Evie to reach them.

"Done," she said.

"You got to the last gap in time?" Juan asked.

"I didn't need to." She explained how Susie had handled the sheep as if she'd done it for years.

Juan was stunned. "How did she know how to do that?"

"I don't know."

"It's because she's the bestest dog in the world." Evie flung her arms around the dog, who wiggled with delight, once again the silly pup. "We ares a team. *Mamm* says it's *gut* to bees a team." Raising her head, she said, "Ain't so, Juan?"

Watching his face, Annalise could see he was torn. He wanted to keep that space between them, but he wouldn't be false with her daughter.

"Ja," he said. "A *gut* team."

He reached out toward Annalise. She grasped his hand, worried he was feeling light-headed. When he squeezed her fingers and smiled, she grinned. Who would have guessed an everyday task like shifting sheep from one field to another would begin to heal the wound that had been festering in her heart before Boaz's death? It was a small step forward, but it was a step, and for that she was grateful.

Juan was nervous about the visit to the *doktor*'s office, and his mouth was incapable of stopping words from spewing out of it as he rode with Annalise toward Montague. They'd dropped Evie and Susie off at her farm, but that didn't halt him from talking about the dog.

"I've said it before and I'll say it again, but what Susie did was amazing."

"Ja, you've said it before." She chuckled as she guided the horse through the roundabout. Cars had whizzed by them on the road, but they fell in line behind the buggy as Annalise drove most of the way around the circle.

He ignored her amusement. "I may want to borrow

her when lambing season comes around. I lost two lambs this year to coyotes. Susie would keep them away."

"You may be right. She's gentle with Evie, and she clearly considers the sheep her responsibility, too." She laughed, and he savored the sound. At first, she had been somber around him, but she laughed as easily with him as she did with her daughter. "She considers everything on your farm and on mine hers."

"True." He recalled petting the dog's head by the gate and wondered how the texture of Susie's fur compared with Annalise's hair.

He silenced the traitorous thoughts that he struggled to keep under control. As soon as he did, anticipation of what could happen at Dr. Armstrong's office filled his head. What did the flashing lights mean? Was it a sign his vision was returning or was it his vision's last gasp effort?

When the buggy was parked and they were walking toward the office's door, he moved his cane in front of him. It hit something, and he tightened his grip on Annalise's arm, halting her.

She gasped. *"Was iss letz?"*

"Nothing is wrong as long as you don't trip over that stone right in front of you."

"There isn't…oh, there it is!"

Stones rattled, and he guessed she'd kicked the offending one aside.

"Danki," she said. "That's great, Juan. You sensed the stone with your cane."

"I'm as surprised as you are."

"Neither of us should be surprised. You've been working hard to get as *gut* as Evie is with a cane."

"She's far more competent than I am, but I'm learning. Thanks to you."

With a sense not among his normal five, he knew she was smiling. He returned it, as he warned himself not to be captivated by his friend's widow. Not as long as his ears could recall Boaz's words about how she could switch from delightful to demanding in a single heartbeat.

You haven't seen any sign of her doing that, not even when you resisted using a cane.

Every day, Annalise was becoming more involved in his life, and every day, he was getting more confused whether that was a *gut* thing or not.

Thoughts of anything but what awaited him in the *doktor*'s office fled when they walked into the waiting room. Annalise went to check in while he sat on an unyielding chair. She didn't have a chance to join him before the nurse called for him to follow her to an examination room.

"You, too, Mrs. Overgard," the nurse said. "Doctor wants to check that cut in your thumb."

They were led to the same room they'd been in two days ago, but this time it was Juan who sat on the examination table while Annalise was relegated to the plastic chair. Neither of them spoke while they waited for Dr. Armstrong to arrive, but he guessed her thoughts matched his as he pondered what being blind for the rest of his life would mean.

Dr. Armstrong came into the room with a warm greeting. As he washed his hands in a sink to Juan's left, he said, "Annalise, let me look at that thumb before I get to Juan." There was silence for a couple of seconds before the *doktor* assured her it was healing and asked, "Do you have any questions?"

"*Ja*, but not about my thumb. Do you know how I

can arrange for our Saint Bernard to be registered as a service dog?"

"Has she had any training?"

"Nothing formal, but she anticipates Evie's every move, making sure she stays where she'll be safe. Summer is coming, and Evie keeps asking to go to the beach. It would be *wunderbaar* to have another set of eyes on her because she wants to explore farther away from me with each passing year."

Another set of eyes? If his worked, then Annalise wouldn't have to ask the *doktor* that question.

This isn't about you! The little voice in Juan's head sounded angry. Angrier than ever.

As his world had narrowed in the hours and days after his accident, he'd sunk into the muck of his own problems. He'd thought of how he could overcome his headaches and how he was unable to see. His world had widened since then, first to his bed, then to his room and the house beyond it. All thanks to Annalise.

"There's no specific identification card you need in Prince Edward Island for a service dog," the *doktor* said. "The province's Human Rights Act provides protection for disabled people, and under its provisions, nobody can be denied reasonable accommodation to help them integrate into society." He chuckled. "Big words that politicians love, but it means if having a service dog will help Evie, she may have one go with her wherever she goes. I do suggest you get the dog a vest to wear, so nobody will bother you with questions about why she's with your daughter."

"Where can I get one?" Annalise asked.

"They're easy to order online." He paused, then said, "I'll have one ordered for you. They usually take a couple of weeks to come in, so it should be here by Victoria

Day if you want to go to the beach then like so many others do. Not me. The water's too cold for me in late May."

"Maybe that will keep Evie from running right out into it."

They laughed together, but Juan couldn't join in. His lungs couldn't draw in much air, and he almost choked on each exhale. It was as if every part of his body had shut down, not just his eyes.

"How are you doing, Juan?" the *doktor* asked.

"I'm seeing things."

"What things?"

"Flashes of light. At the corners of my eyes. If I look at them, they vanish. Does that mean my sight is coming back?" The words exploded out of him as hard as the steam tank had sent shrapnel across the barnyard.

Dr. Armstrong's voice was neutral. "Flashes often accompany migraines. Have you been having worse headaches?"

"No. In fact, my head's been aching less with each passing day."

"That's good. Let's take a look."

Juan held still as the *doktor* leaned closer to examine his eyes. The brush of air against his face was a combination of the other man's breath and the movement of the ophthalmoscope that gave the *doktor* a better view into Juan's eyes.

Dr. Armstrong sighed. "I don't see any change. Your eyes appear normal."

"But I can't see anything." Repeating the words he'd said in desperation the day of the explosion had been the last thing Juan had wanted to do. Yet, it was as if his emotions were as useless as his eyes. An odd numbness claimed him and left him disconnected from the situation. Had his brain endured the most it could and refused to deal with any more bad news? "I can't see anything but flashes."

"What does that mean, Dr. Armstrong?" Annalise's voice was taut with dismay.

How could she be more upset than he was? That was wrong. Why did he feel nothing?

Whatever else was said in the examination room went right past the weird buzzing in his ears. He replied to questions he thought were being asked, but couldn't care if his answers made sense or not. When the *doktor* put a hand on his arm and gave a gentle tug to alert him it was time to get down, he complied. He followed Annalise out of the room, out of the building and across the parking lot.

The sun heated his face, but it might as well have been the foggiest possible day because he couldn't see anything. Even the flashes had deserted him.

He was numb. More than when he'd opened his eyes after the explosion and hadn't been able to see. Then he'd been filled with curiosity about what had happened and healing. Reality had arrived, leaving him feeling as if he'd been through dental work with an anesthesia that refused to wear off. Trepidation taunted him, warning him that if he relinquished an iota of the numbness, the pain would be overwhelming.

In the buggy, he was silent. Annalise was as well until they'd driven through the tight curve of the round-about and onto the road leading north.

"How are you doing?" she asked.

"How do you think?" His voice remained dull in spite of his sarcasm.

"It was a silly question," she said, her tone calm. "You're in shock, Juan."

"It's not a bad place to be. If I linger here, I don't have to think about the what-ifs."

"What-ifs?"

"What if my vision never returns?"

"You shouldn't think that way."

A truck sped past, and Juan waited until its thunder had receded into the distance. "You're the one who tells me I have to be realistic and prepare to handle my limitations."

"Realistic, not pessimistic. You're acting as if you don't have the greatest ally on your side."

"Ally?"

"God."

He almost snorted in derision. If God was on his side, why had He let the tractor blow up when Juan stood within range?

As if he'd asked that question aloud, Annalise said, "I know you're angry at God for what happened, but have you considered that you could have been killed that day? God put His hand between you and the worst of the flying debris, so you didn't lose your life."

"Only my sight." His mouth tightened so much he had to force each word past his lips. "Don't tell me I should be grateful that was all I lost. All? You've got no idea what it's like to go from seeing everything one minute to seeing nothing the next."

"I don't understand what it's like." She shifted on the seat, and he wondered if she was facing him. "I'm blessed I can admit that, but I'll also admit that neither you nor me or anyone else knows what God has planned for you. Your sight may come back. It may not. You've got two more weeks before that six-week deadline."

"Not much time."

"It may be enough. Whatever happens will happen

on God's timeline, not yours or mine or anyone else's in this world."

"So you're saying I have to be patient."

"No!" Her shoulder brushed his, and he sensed the tension she'd kept out of her voice. "Patience doesn't have anything to do with it. It's faith and acceptance. I was angry with God when I learned Evie was blind, that she'd never see anything. So many things I'd imagined us doing together seemed impossible."

"What things?"

"Reading books and sewing and baking and working in the garden."

"She does most of those things."

"All of them. But at the time, I couldn't imagine that. It was as if there'd been a terrible death in the family. Instead of celebrating and praising God I had an otherwise healthy *boppli*, I thought about what I wouldn't have with her."

"You got those things."

"On God's timeline, not mine. You've got two more weeks, Juan. Don't throw those days away by sinking into depression again."

"Again?"

She didn't answer right away, and when she did, her voice was hushed. "I know you've been curious why I wanted to talk to Dr. Armstrong alone earlier this week."

"I was for a short while." That wasn't quite true. He still wondered what she'd wanted to talk to the *doktor* about in private.

"I talked to him about you and how depressed you've been. How you've been seeing the worst possible outcome of every event. I wanted advice on how to cheer you up when you're feeling so down, so everything doesn't look so dark."

He gave a terse laugh as she turned the buggy onto the road leading toward Georgetown and their farms. "Everything I see is dark, including the future." He hated his whining, but he wouldn't lie and he wouldn't admit the truth.

"You can't know the future, but God can."

"I wish He'd tell me." He meant the words as a derisive joke, but then realized it was the truth. If he had an inkling his sight would return, it would be easier to endure.

Wouldn't it?

"That's where faith comes in, Juan. Believing God has a plan for us. You know that in your heart. Seek in your heart, and you'll find God waiting there for you."

"Is that what you did after Boaz died?"

Her voice caught. "*Ja*. That frightful night when Boaz didn't come home and the more frightful days that followed. I leaned on our Heavenly Father, and He gave me comfort because I knew no matter what else happened, He would never desert me, and He hasn't deserted you."

"It feels that way."

"I know, but reach out for Him, and you'll find He has been there all along. Faith isn't about seeing Him. It's about feeling Him standing beside you when you wonder how you can take another step."

"You've been there for me, Annalise, when I've felt that way."

She put her hand on his arm and squeezed it. "I'm glad I've been able to, but you need to turn to God more than you've turned to me. He knows what lies ahead for you and is there to help you through every minute of every day. I've been praying that someday soon, you won't need my help."

Juan knew she meant her words to be bolstering, but they had the opposite effect. What would happen when, one day, she told him she'd taught him everything she could? He'd be without her teasing and coercing him to do his exercises to become more independent and also without her soft, kind words and touch that made his heart sing.

Alone. As he once had believed he wanted. He'd been wrong.

Chapter Twelve

Juan shouldn't have been surprised when the skills Annalise had taught him worked while he made his lunch for the first time since the explosion.

Carrying a glass of water to the table, he put it on the mat near the plate holding his grilled cheese sandwich. He was proud of making the sandwich and only burning himself twice. It was an improvement over the last time he'd tried under Annalise's supervision. Before he was blinded, he'd scorched his fingers almost every time he'd cooked the sandwich. Usually because he was too eager to eat it before the bubbling cheese cooled off.

He pulled out a chair and eased down onto it as he leaned his cane against the table. He held his hand near the cane, but it didn't move or tip over as it had when he'd first started using it.

Was he becoming accustomed to being blind? Or more accepting that his circumstances might be God's will? After his visit to the *doktor*'s office last week, he'd spent a lot of time talking to God. He hadn't tried to curb his fury. Instead, he'd let it out, being up-front with his Heavenly Father as Annalise had urged. He'd ranted. He'd shouted. He'd cried out his frustration, shaking his fists and stamping about the house until every ounce of his rage had been vented. Into the emptiness left behind, he welcomed the sense of peace he'd forgotten.

Self-doubts and anger lingered at the edge of his mind, but he tried to keep them out of his thoughts. Instead of dreading the difficulties of the day, he would try to take each as it came. He wouldn't think of how much he'd lost, but what he could gain in the future.

More than a week remained in the countdown to that critical date after his accident. Annalise had assured him yesterday that Dr. Armstrong had said more than once that nobody should take that month and a half as an exact drop-dead deadline.

Each person, each situation is unique, was how she'd put it. *Don't surrender to despair while you've got hope.*

A knock on the door broke into Juan's thoughts. Before he could react, the door opened, and he heard the bishop's jovial voice. "Anyone home?"

"Ja," Juan called. "Having a sandwich in the kitchen."

Rodney's work boots thudded against the floor as he walked in. He didn't wait for an invitation, but drew out a chair on the other side of the table and sat.

"What can I do for you, Rodney?" He took a hasty bite of his sandwich, not wanting to let it get cold. Grilled cheese congealed into something that resembled the texture of a rubber mat as it lost its warmth.

"I figured it's past time for me to visit and check on how you're doing, Juan."

"This is a busy time of year."

Rodney's smile wove through his words. "Every time of year is busy for farmers, ain't so? Your fields are looking *gut.*"

"Thanks to my family and other members of the *Leit.*

Without the community, I'd be growing acres of weeds instead of potatoes."

"Jesus urged us to love one another as He loves us. A way we show that love is by helping each other. Something you know because you have offered a hand to others when they needed it. It's your turn to receive those blessings."

"I would have preferred to skip my turn," he said.

The bishop chuckled, and Juan thought about how Rodney's beard wafted across his chest when he laughed. "I'm sure you would have. Mind if I make a sandwich? That smells *gut*."

"Help yourself." He continued eating while the bishop cooked, talking about the latest news from the community.

When a second sandwich slid onto his plate, Juan thanked Rodney and took a careful bite to avoid burning his mouth with the hot cheese.

"Delicious," Rodney said from the other side of the table, "if I say so myself. Is this cheese made by the Lampels?"

"I don't know. Mattie brought me a couple bags of food from the farm shop. All she told me was, 'Here's cheese.'"

With another laugh, the bishop said, "Whoever made it did a *gut* job. Speaking of jobs, how has Annalise been handling the one I gave her?"

"Fine," he replied, knowing that question was the real reason for Rodney's visit. "Better than fine. Annalise and Evie have been doing everything they can to convince this hardheaded man to listen." He locked his hands around his water glass. "Their dogs have being trying to help, though that pug is more helpful in allowing me to practice not tripping over her."

Rodney laughed. "I'm glad to hear everyone, even the smallest members of our community, are doing what they can to assist you on your way to recovery." He paused to take another bite of his sandwich. "I wasn't sure how you'd take Annalise's suggestions."

"I wasn't either, but she's sensible and so are her suggestions. What she's learned from helping Evie is helping me."

"You don't know how happy I am to hear you say that, too."

"You asked Annalise already?"

He could almost hear the bishop shrug. "I wanted to hear your opinion. It's no secret you two haven't always seen eye to eye."

"True."

"Have you patched up things?"

Juan started to say that they had, but paused. Had they put aside their differences? Was it possible if she blamed Juan for her husband's death? She'd never said, and he'd been careful not to ask. His guilt surged forth like a tidal wave, and he shifted on his chair. He knew Rodney was watching, looking for any sign of his thoughts. The bishop always did that when speaking to a member of the *Leit*.

"Things are better," Juan said. "I appreciate what she's done for me, and she appreciates how seriously I take her lessons."

"That's *gut*."

He expected Rodney to ask another probing question, but the bishop returned to talking about crops and what a dry summer would mean to the farmers. When the older man left a half hour later, after having a second grilled cheese sandwich, Juan wasn't sure if he'd answered Rodney's question to the bishop's satisfaction or not.

All he felt in the wake of the bishop's visit was dissatisfaction and uncertainty. He and Annalise had become a team working toward his independence. Could he put aside his guilt over Boaz's death enough to welcome her into his heart as it pleaded with each beat?

He didn't know. That guilt was so much a part of him he wasn't sure what he'd be without it.

"Would you rather be without your guilt or without Annalise in your life?" he mused aloud.

If he let go of his guilt, he would be losing the final connection he had to his friend. If he didn't grasp on to a chance of a life with Annalise, he would lose what might be his final connection to love.

The answer should have been simple, but it wasn't.

The workshop in the small outbuilding in the shadow of the cow barn was Annalise's sanctuary where she could forget about the past and not worry about the future. Here, she could be in the moment because it was where she felt closest to God as she took the gifts of His hands—wood and tools and imagination—to make something *wunderbaar*. Her efforts were simple compared to what God had wrought, but creating a small object helped her understand how God had looked upon the world he'd made and found it *gut*.

Plain folk abhorred *hochmut*, trying to keep from being proud about their accomplishments. At the same time, doing a job well was a goal to aspire to in every part of their lives. It never had made sense to her because she was proud of her little wooden boats and animals, though she never would have said so in front of others.

It'd been too long since she'd last stolen a couple of hours to work in the shop. She hadn't realized how much she missed her haven until she stepped into the woodworking shop and closed the door behind her.

This afternoon, Evie was busy in the house along with *Grossmammi* Fern and the two dogs. The only sound was the rumble of a plank going through the planer. The noise was muted by the headphones Annalise wore. When the board finished emerging on the other side of the planer, she switched the machine off. After she'd removed her hearing protection, she cut the board into pieces, each no bigger than twelve centimeters square. She lifted off the headphones, making sure that her cone-shaped *kapp* stayed in place. She always added extra pins to hold it on her head while in her woodworking shop.

She smiled as she stacked the small chunks of wood on her worktable. This was her happy place. She'd seen a sign at a shop in Shushan, the village at the head of Shushan Bay on the other side of the peninsula, with those words. She made her own sign from a broken pallet. She'd painted the boards black and used bright yellow for the words: Annalise's Happy Place. Looking at the sign always made her grin because it was the truth. Being with her daughter was the only thing that made her happier than being in her woodshop.

Seeing Juan improving makes me happy, too.

With each big step forward with her and Evie's guidance, she'd wanted to celebrate. How could she when his sight hadn't returned? Festivities seemed premature when his prayers hadn't been answered.

Was he praying?

Annalise paused as she stepped around the machine to switch it off. Each time she'd mentioned God, Juan had closed up like a vault. What he wasn't saying told her so much. He believed God wasn't listening to his prayers. When Evie had prayed and hadn't gotten the answer she wanted, Annalise had explained that sometimes God's answer was no. How could she say that to Juan? There was a huge difference between praying for an extra piece of chocolate cake and the restoration of one's vision.

Sending up a prayer for healing for him, she reminded herself this time was for her and her work. She'd been ignoring it while helping Juan, and she needed to make more projects to sell. The wood block was smooth. She'd cut it into a small horse. Tourists snatched them up as if they were painted with gold instead of simple latex paint. The money had helped buy shoes and other things they couldn't grow or make on the farm.

A knock sounded on her door, and she flinched, her fingers bumping the boats. Two fell onto the floor. She scooped them up and deposited them on the table before she rushed to the door. Who was knocking? She wished she could will the person on the other side to go away. She didn't want anyone in her private space today.

Throwing the door open, she gasped when she saw Juan. Surprise put an edge on her voice. "What are you doing here? Did you *komm* alone? *Was iss letz?*"

"One question at a time," he said with a grin. "You sound like Evie." She started to reply, but he held up a hand. "In reverse order, there's nothing wrong. No, I didn't *komm* here on my own. Mattie drove me here because she was heading this way anyhow to deliver some fabric to Chalonna."

She knew he meant Chalonna Lampel, who lived a kilometer up the road. "You haven't answered my first question," she said as she guided him into the workshop, but not far. Dangerous tools were locked away or mostly unplugged, but the small barn was a maze. "What are you doing here?"

"Can't a guy pay a call on his neighbors to see how they're doing without it being a big deal?"

"If that guy ever had in the past."

He winced. "Guess a visit is long overdue, ain't so?"

She wasn't fooled by his casual tone. "Let me unplug a couple of things," she said, "and we can go into the house. *Grossmammi* Fern and Evie were frosting a chocolate cake with pecan-coconut frosting when I came out. I'm sure they're ready to share it."

He put out his arm, blocking her way. "I'd rather have a tour of your woodworking shop. I used to hear the whine of your tools, and I've been curious what you're doing in here. What do you make?"

"Toys and trinkets. Nothing very valuable."

"I find that hard to believe. I heard Mattie trying to convince you to sell your pieces at the farm shop. She wouldn't be saying that unless she thought your work was *gut*. Very *gut*."

"They're things tourists can find room for in their luggage and display to help them remember their trip to the Island. Coasters with quilt designs painted on them, little animals, things like that."

"What can I do to help?" Juan asked.

Astonished, she asked, "You want to help me?"

"Why not?" He smiled, and that familiar warmth bubbled in her center. "You've helped me so much. Shouldn't I return the favor?"

"I didn't help you because I expected something in return." Her voice was gruff as she tried to silence her reaction to his smile.

"I know that. You helped me because Rodney ordered you to."

"He didn't order me. Not exactly." She added the last to be honest.

He laughed. "Rodney can make his orders sound like requests."

"True." Letting the tension slide off her shoulders, she said, "I'll give you something to do while I finish up my project." She hurried on before he could ask what it was. "Then we'll sample the cake *Grossmammi* Fern and Evie made."

"I like that plan."

"I thought you might." Pulling a stool beside her worktable, she told him to sit there.

Annalise picked up one of the small wooden horses she'd cut out. Taking his hand, she put the rough horse on his palm.

"You can start with sanding this," she said. "Be careful. There are plenty of slivers on it."

"What is it?" he asked as he balanced the horse.

"It's a dala horse."

His brows lowered in a frown. "Dala? I've never heard of that breed."

She laughed. "It's not a real horse. It's a simple form that was developed in a part of Sweden called Dalarna. Horses were as important to the ancient Scandinavians as they are to us. They were respected for their strength and courage. These little horses, which are often painted bright red, were made as toys by furniture makers who had leftover wood. I make them because I like their shape and so do tourists."

"Are these what Mattie wants to add to her inventory at the farm shop?"

"These and a couple of the other things I make." She

handed him a small piece of sandpaper and explained how he should run it along the grain of the piece.

"How can I tell which way that is?" he asked.

"I'll start you off. Once you get it a bit smoother, you can feel the direction of the grain with your fingertips."

Stepping behind him, she took his hand holding the sandpaper and demonstrated. Or tried to because she couldn't ignore how strong his hand was beneath hers and how broad his shoulders were as she leaned over them to guide his hand. Wisps of his hair brushed her cheek, and she longed to close her eyes and savor being so close to a handsome man.

"I think I've got it," he said, jerking her to reality with the realization he must not have felt the same connection she had.

Stop fooling yourself, she said. *To him, you're his teacher. His reluctant teacher.*

She left him to his task while she returned to hers. She'd thought she'd learned her lesson with Boaz, but she hadn't. She wished she'd never opened her workshop door and let Juan into her space that was no longer a haven from the past.

Juan was amazed. For once, he and Annalise weren't locking horns. She was working on the other side of the table while he sanded the small horse on his side. He was aware of every motion she made, the *skritch* sound of the sandpaper she used, the way she blew out her breath in a determined sigh as she bent to rub harder, how she became silent before setting an item on the table. He guessed she was examining her work to see if it met her standards.

As she had while teaching him to use his cane. Had she seen that as rubbing off his rough edges?

He bent his head, not wanting her to see his grin and ask what he was thinking.

I'm thinking of you. How would she react if he told her that she was on his mind all the time?

"Looking *gut*," Annalise said, and he realized he hadn't noticed her coming around the table to stand by him.

"*Danki*, Annalise."

"I should be the one thanking you."

"For doing one horse in the time it took you to sand more than a half dozen."

Surprise heightened her voice. "How did you know?"

"I heard you pick up and put down each one." He reached to touch the wooden designs in the middle of the table. "These aren't horses. They're boats. Lobster boats."

"You're figuring things out when you touch them."

"The shape of a lobster boat is pretty unique."

"And simple."

"Why are you making these shapes? After…"

She didn't answer for a long minute, then said, "Tourists like them."

He caught her arm as she'd been turning away. "How can *you* make these little boats? They've got to remind you of Boaz."

"It's not like I ever forget him, Juan." She drew her hand out of his arm.

He let her go, not wanting to press further. Had he really thought that she'd put Boaz in her past simply because Juan couldn't stop thinking about her? She'd been married to Boaz and had a *kind* with him. That her husband hadn't been honest with her the last months of his life didn't erase what they'd shared.

Did it?

Confused, Juan put the little boat on the table, trying not to knock off the others. He was relieved when he managed it. When she walked away, returning to where she'd been working, he was disappointed. He'd hoped their conversation would continue.

He started to speak, but shut his mouth as the door opened. He recognized the footfalls before Annalise said, "Evie, you know you're not supposed to *komm* in here without permission."

Patting Susie's head, he hoped the dog's wagging tail wouldn't knock against the equipment. As he thought that, something hit the floor with a clang.

"*Komm mol*, Susie," he said, grabbing the Saint Bernard by the scruff. "Out you go."

The dog went with Juan, but when he closed the door she whined her dismay. Leaning against the door, he realized by the scent of Annalise's rose-scented shampoo that she stood not far away.

"*Grossmammi* Fern says I shoulds talks to you, *Mamm*." The little girl sounded bewildered. "Permissing, ain't so?"

Annalise relented enough to say, "You need to get *permission* from me, and no dogs in here at any time. They could get hurt."

"Okays. Next times."

"*Ja.* Now, what's so important that you asked *Grossmammi* Fern if you could come out here? Is it because the cake is done?"

"Cake is dones, but you saids we could goes to the beach on Vic's Day, ain't so?"

"*Ja.*" She added under her breath so only he'd hear. "She's talking about Victoria Day."

"I got that," Juan answered.

"Vic's Day is Monday," Evie said. "We goes to beach?"

"*Ja*, as long as you promise to stay with me and not wander away."

"Evie stays with you. Susie stays with you."

He could imagine Annalise's forehead threading with dismay when she said, "I don't know if Susie can go to the beach. Some beaches don't allow dogs." Her voice brightened. "Except service dogs."

Evie grasped his sleeve. "Juan goes, too?"

"If your *mamm* doesn't mind," he said, wondering how the little girl's innocent words could make his heart beat faster as he imagined spending the day with Annalise.

Just what she needs, his mind berated him. *A blind man to take care of in addition to her blind kind. If you cared for her as much as you claim you do, you'd get out of her life.*

"Juan is welcome to join us," Annalise said before he could find a way to bow out graciously. "Getting more fresh air would be *gut* for all of us."

Did she have to try hard to sound as if she was being genuine? "We could have a great time," he said. "If Susie's service dog vest is available in time, it would be a *gut* opportunity to see how she acts in a crowd."

"It could be a big crowd," Annalise warned. "Lots of people have the day off."

"The water is too cold to swim, so that will cut down on the number there. With so many beaches in Prince Edward Island, there's bound to be room for everyone."

"If we go to Georgetown—"

"That beach is on the river rather than the ocean," he reminded her.

"We goes to the ocean," Evie interjected. "Wants to goes to the ocean."

"There are two votes for the ocean." Juan chuckled.

Juan guessed Annalise was frowning. "I didn't realize this was a democracy."

"Which ocean beach would you suggest?" he asked, ignoring her sarcasm.

Evie spoke before Annalise could. "Wants to goes to the Singing Sands beach."

"Where's that?" he asked. "I don't think I've heard of that beach."

Annalise answered, "It's Basin Head Provincial Park. The sand there has quartz in it. When the grains rub together, they make a soft humming sound. No, it's not a hum, but it's a sound. More like a squeak."

"We goes there?" asked Evie.

"On Monday, I'll hire Max to take us to the beach." She added, "It's sixty kilometers from here, so too far to go by buggy."

Evie squealed and ran out to head back to the house.

As Annalise closed the door, she said, "You're welcome to join us, Juan, but if you don't want to—"

"How can I resist hearing a whole beach sing?"

"Don't expect music. It's more like the sound of sandpaper on wood."

"It should be fascinating."

"*Gut.* I'll let you know when we'll be leaving once I speak with Max."

He could tell that she was hoping he'd be on his way. "I'll bring sunscreen. Don't want anyone to get burned."

"*Danki.*"

His fingers followed the sound of her voice and touched her cheek. She edged away.

"What are you doing?" she asked.

"Trying to see you."

"You don't need to examine my face. You know what I look like."

"Most of the times I saw you, you were wearing a frown."

She laughed. "Caused by something you'd said."

"True, but I'd like to *see* you with a smile. May I?"

"All right," she whispered as if she didn't trust her voice.

He reached across the narrow space between them and found her cheek. Her skin was soft and smoother than the wooden horse he'd sanded with care. Wisps of hair edged her forehead, which wrinkled beneath his touch. He jerked back his fingers.

"Sorry," she murmured. "It's been a while since Evie did this, and I'm out of practice. I'll try to be still."

"It's okay," he said. "I know this is an invasion of your private space."

"It isn't. I've been the one to tell others it's fine when Evie wants to 'see' them."

"If you're sure…"

She took his hand and drew it toward her face. "I'm sure."

Was he sure? He wondered if this chance would come again if he backed away. He brushed his fingertips across her lips. His whole hand tingled as he imagined him kissing her instead of mapping her face with his fingers. When her breath caressed his skin, he knew inhaling was impossible. His other hand rose toward her waist to draw her closer.

He forced both of his hands away from her. If he stood there a heartbeat longer, he wouldn't be able to keep from kissing her.

Somehow, he found the door and opened it. He stumbled out and took a single step, then froze. He'd left his cane inside her workshop. To go in… He didn't have the strength to resist her if they stood face-to-face.

"Here." Annalise's voice was unsteady as she pressed his cane into his hand. "You'll need this."

I need you, he wanted to retort, but halted the words he must never speak as he crossed the yard, heading toward the road where he would be able to flag down Mattie on her return. He sensed Annalise was watching him, but he didn't turn or speak. What could he say other than he'd fallen in love with his friend's widow and he had no idea how to fall *out* of love with her?

Chapter Thirteen

The beach far down the hill from the parking lot was busy, and Annalise smiled as her daughter chattered nonstop. She didn't glance at Juan, who'd been quiet during the drive to Basin Head Provincial Park. Not that he would have had a chance to get in a word while Evie exclaimed about how special Susie was to have a service dog vest and asked how much longer would it take to reach the beach. When they'd turned on the road that led to the parking lot, only the little girl's seat belt had kept her from floating to the top of the van with her excitement.

The lot was full, so Max had stopped near the building with showers and changing rooms. They weren't the only ones eager to celebrate Victoria Day and the *wunderbaar* sunny day. After two days of chilly spring weather in the teens, the temperature was already nearing the midtwenties. A few cottony clouds broke the brilliant blue sky.

Annalise helped Evie out and moved aside as Susie jumped down. She noticed people glancing at them. Dogs weren't always welcome at the provincial beaches, but Dr. Armstrong had been as *gut* as his word and made sure they had a bright red vest with the words *Service Dog* embroidered on it. He'd found a distributor that had a vest large enough for a half–Saint Bernard.

Susie looked dignified wearing the vest…other than the drool that always marked her path. Evie had been delighted to discover the vest had pockets, and she'd decided to fill them with her favorite candy bars and small bottles of water and fruit juice. When Annalise had reminded her that there was a café at the beach, Evie had announced the provisions she'd packed were for "emergencies."

She shouldn't have read Evie the story about Saint Bernards rescuing travelers in the Alps. Evie had decided Susie should have every opportunity to prove she could be a heroine. Her daughter had listened when Annalise had reminded Evie that an emergency must be real and must be avoided.

"Otherwise," Annalise had said, "anyone could be a heroine and it's not special anymore. Let's let God decide when Susie should be a heroine."

The little girl had agreed, but Annalise knew she needed to keep a close eye on Evie and the dog.

Once Juan had emerged from the van and Annalise collected the wicker basket holding what they'd need for the day, Max wished them a *gut* time. "I'll pick you up around three," the driver said. "I've got several errands to do on this end of the Island, so that should work out well."

Annalise thanked him and took Evie's hand. She waited for her daughter and Juan to position their canes, then led the way away from the parking lot and toward the water. As she approached the edge of the lot, she could see water sparkling at the bottom of the hill. She glanced at the wooden stairs that led down to the boardwalk. They were steep and uneven. It might be better to use the gravel road. The wheelchair access symbol on the gate at the top of the road reassured her about her decision.

"We're going down a hill to reach the beach," she said as she put Juan's hand on her upper arm. She smiled when her daughter reached out to grasp Susie's bright red vest. "We're going slow. No running. I don't want anyone to end up on their nose at the bottom of the hill."

"Ouch," Evie said as she touched her nose. "Don't dos that!"

"A *gut* idea," Annalise replied. "Let's go slowly."

About halfway down, as others hurried past them, Juan asked, "How far away is the beach?"

"We're about halfway to the buildings along the cliff," she said, understanding his concern. They kept to a deliberate pace while she kept an eye on Evie and him as well as Susie. People shied away from the big dog, afraid they'd get bitten if they got too close. She wanted to reassure them, but had to concentrate on getting everyone down the hill without falling. "There's a flat boardwalk that should make it easier for us. It leads to the beach."

He nodded. "I had no idea we'd be walking down the side of a mountain."

"A hill, but a vertical one."

He edged away. His shoe slid in the gravel, but he didn't lose his footing. "I'd better make haste slowly." When he laughed, her shoulders relaxed.

She hadn't realized how tense she'd become while he sat in the van like a statue, saying nothing. She wasn't sure why he'd left her workshop so abruptly three days ago, and she'd be wise not to ask. Instead, she wanted to enjoy the day, the sunshine and the beach.

At the bottom where the road curved, Annalise waited until Evie and Juan had stepped onto the boardwalk. When her daughter stomped her feet, Evie tilted her head, listening for the echo of the wood beneath her.

"Not singing?" she asked.

"Those are the boards, not the sand," Annalise answered.

"Sands on the boards."

Juan guffawed. "She's right, Annalise."

"*Ja.* She is." Taking her daughter's hand, she said, "We've got the boardwalk for a short distance, and then we'll be walking on plastic mats through the sand." She kept up the description as they strolled past buildings where she could see another shower and storage for equipment for the lifeguards and maintenance crew. "There's a channel with a bridge across it. The channel is flanked by walls that are flush with the walk to the beach. Signs are posted not to jump off the walls or the bridge."

A loud splash sounded, and Juan and Evie looked at her, confused.

"People are ignoring the signs," Annalise said, "and the lifeguards are letting them as long as they don't do anything too dangerous. Oh!"

"What is it?" Juan asked as another splash sent water flying to the top of the wall.

"A kid did a backflip off the bridge into the channel."

"It's called a run," he said.

"The current?"

"No, the river going from the harbor out into the ocean. Those are known as runs on the Island."

"I didn't know that."

He smiled. "I've finally got the chance to teach you something. Feels *gut*."

"You taught us how to move sheep."

Stretching out his hand, he patted Susie's head. "At least one of you had it figured out already."

As they neared the side of the run, Annalise slowed. She didn't want to chance any of them falling over the side. She could swim and assumed Susie was able to, but Evie couldn't. Could Juan?

"The current goes fast through the run," she said. "It's carrying people from the inner harbor right beneath the bridge and out into the ocean."

"Sounds like fun." His eyes glittered with amusement.

"Maybe, but not for us. We don't have anything to wear into the water."

"That sounds as if you planned for that on purpose."

"*Ja*. We'll have to save it for our next trip, ain't so?"

"Me, too?" asked Evie.

"Everyone riding the current is old enough to go to school," Annalise replied.

Her daughter's mouth twisted into a pout. "I wants to go."

"When you're big enough to go to school, we'll talk about it."

"Okays."

Annalise turned their group to the right and onto the smaller beach that was edged by red cliffs. The rocks looked like mounds of red velvet cake pressed between the green grass at the top and the lighter sand along the beach.

Once they found an empty spot above the tide line, Annalise opened the basket and drew out a blanket. She spread it on the sand and sat on one corner. Juan sat on the other side, then yelped as he was hit by sand when Evie and Susie went racing along the beach.

Annalise ran and caught up to her daughter and the dog. Apologizing to people who'd gotten splattered with sand, she marched them back to where Juan was spitting.

"That'll teach me to leave my mouth open," he said.

"Sorry," Evie said before being prompted.

"Play here," Annalise said. "You and Susie can dig and see what you can find."

"Wants sands to sing."

"Move your feet back and forth in the sand and be very quiet. You should be able to hear it."

Annalise saw her daughter's frustration when she couldn't pick up the sound out of the noise around them.

"Sit, Evie," she said, pulling off her sneakers and socks. "Listen hard."

As she rubbed her own feet against the sand, she saw her daughter's face lighten with a grin.

"I hears it!"

She put her finger to the little girl's lips. "Shh. Listen."

Scooting her feet around in a small circle, she smiled when Evie began to clap along with the motion she couldn't have seen. She must be hearing more than Annalise did.

"Likes singing sands," Evie announced. She spread her fingers in the sand and picked up a mussel shell. "Gots something! What is it?"

Annalise explained what the shell was as well as the other items Evie dug from the sand. When Juan taught her daughter how to make a sandcastle, Annalise watched, smiling. Susie lay in the sand, cooling herself as the sun rose higher in the sky. Shouts of excitement came from the bridge as more kids and a few adults jumped off. When the tide slid out, a sandbar appeared on the other side of the run about ten meters out from the beach. It soon was filled with people excited about being on dry land with the ocean on every side, albeit a shallow ocean.

Others went to the café at the top of the hill, but Annalise was glad she'd brought peanut butter and jelly sandwiches for them. Susie's was just peanut butter, and she ate with the same gusto Evie did.

Finishing his, Juan said, "That may have been the best sandwich I've ever eaten."

"Everything tastes better by the water." Annalise laughed as she wiped crumbs off her apron and held out the bag of potato chips.

He took a handful and ate them. Leaning back on his elbows, he said, "I've been remiss in not taking time to visit the beaches. I need to start wandering around more."

"Get your wandering in before winter." She laughed. "I wouldn't want to sit here in January."

The conversation remained light as they finished their meal. Evie spent more time building a mound which she dubbed Castle Susie, but began to yawn. When Annalise urged her to stretch out on the blanket, she did, taking up almost every centimeter because Susie plopped down next to her, spraying the whole area with sand.

Juan leaped aside, and Annalise edged away as quickly. Standing, she offered him her arm. She led him closer to the cliffs where walking was easier. She didn't want to go far because Evie would be frightened if she woke in an unfamiliar place alone.

They sat on two boulders. Annalise stared out at the motion of the waves. In a storm it would be wild, but today it was gentle.

"When the water is like this," she mused, "I can understand its fascination for Boaz."

"I didn't expect to hear you say that."

"Why?" When he didn't answer right away, she said, "Sorry. I shouldn't have asked that. Somehow, you got in the middle of our troubles, and that wasn't right."

"It wasn't intentional," he said.

Her eyes widened when she realized he thought she was accusing him of planting himself between her and Boaz. Why wouldn't he? She'd said pretty much that to him more than once before Boaz's death.

Stretching, she took his hand and folded it between hers. "Juan, you're misunderstanding me. I didn't mean that you decided to come between us. Rather I meant you were placed there without your choice. I don't know if I put you there first or Boaz, and it doesn't matter any longer. Neither of us should have dumped our problems on your doorstep." She released his fingers as she clasped her hands around her knee. "Boaz was frustrated with me."

"No kidding."

She smiled. "*Ja*, no kidding. I knew when I married him he had big dreams. What I didn't know was how often those dreams would change."

"What do you mean?" His brows shot upward along with the question.

"First, he wanted a farm. He couldn't talk about anything else. In fact, when he found out I was going to have a *boppli*, he grew more eager to have a farm. He decided we'd move to Prince Edward Island because farmland was available here. Without consulting me, he made the down payment on our farm. I didn't know about it until he told me I needed to start packing because we were moving the following week."

"That sounds like Boaz. Once he gets…once he *got* his mind wrapped around something, he couldn't be budged from it." His voice dropped to almost a whisper. "Like the day when he decided he was going out on the lobster boat. He refused to reconsider when I told him I couldn't go that day, but I'd be able to go the following week."

"The lobster season was over the next week."

"I know that now."

She nodded, then recalling how he couldn't see the motion, she said, "I don't know why he changed from wanting to be a farmer to wanting to be a lobsterman. He never explained it to me. Did he explain it to you?"

"He got excited talking about boats. He went on about being out to sea where it would be him and the elements, and he'd be able to prove he had what it took."

"To do that, all he needed to do was stay on the farm and be a *daed* for his daughter. He wouldn't do that, and I couldn't forgive him for turning his back on us. I pushed him away when I should have been insisting he stick closer. Maybe if I'd been different, he wouldn't have been so eager to run away from us."

Juan wished there was something he could say to ease the grief and guilt lying on Annalise's heart. If he spoke the truth that he'd come to believe Boaz had been thinking only of himself when he tossed aside everything, she might be hurt further.

"It wasn't you, Annalise," he said. "You didn't make him leave that day. I don't think he was running away as much as he was running toward what he believed was out there waiting for him."

"What was that?"

He shrugged. "I don't know. If he'd become a lobsterman, how long would that have satisfied him? What would he have decided to try next? I can't tell you because he never told me."

"*Danki* for being honest with me, Juan," she said.

"I've always tried to be honest with you. I thought you knew after my bellyaching in the wake of the accident."

"You didn't complain…too much."

Chuckling, he said, "I complained a lot, and you put up with it."

"You were angry and frightened."

"I didn't want to be frightened. I wanted to find a solution to what was slowing me down and move on with my life. I…"

Juan squinted, then opened his eyes wide. Nothing changed. For the first time since the tractor had exploded, he saw something beyond a gray nothingness lit by sparks. What was he seeing? Darker lumps and lighter expanses. More sparkles. Were they something real or his eyes struggling with the damage done to them?

"Was iss letz?" Annalise asked. "Juan, something is wrong. What?"

"Just a second."

Standing, he turned in one direction and then the other. He listened for the sound of the waves. When he was facing them, he closed his eyes, then opened them.

The lighter expanse in front of him appeared larger. He cut his eyes to his left. The dark nuggets were there, rising from the level of his feet to far above his head.

"Juan, what is it? Are you okay?"

Instead of answering her, he asked, "The cliffs are to my left, ain't so?"

"Ja."

He faced the opposite direction. "There's something on the top of the cliffs straight ahead."

"*Ja.* It's a gazebo up near the café and gift shop."

Continuing to turn, he pointed across the beach. "The sea is that way. From there to…there where the cliffs begin."

"*Ja.*" Excitement made her voice raise. "Can you see that, or are you guessing?"

"I see shadows. Nothing more. Lighter shadows and darker shadows."

"Oh, *danki*, God!" she cried, throwing her arms around his shoulders.

He pulled her closer and leaned his cheek against hers. Shutting his eyes, he held her for a pair of heartbeats before he raised his head and opened his eyes.

The light and dark shadows were still there.

He must have said that aloud because Annalise said, "We've got to get you to Dr. Armstrong's office. Let me collect Evie and Susie and our stuff."

"Max won't be here for an hour or two."

"I'll borrow someone's phone and call him." She grabbed his arms. "Pray, Juan. Pray this is the beginning of your vision coming back."

He nodded, but she'd already released him. He heard her asking someone for their phone, explaining Juan needed to see a *doktor* right away.

More quickly than he would have guessed possible, Juan was being herded up the hill as if he was one of his sheep. Susie followed close on his heels, and Evie chirped like an overwrought squirrel, asking questions in swift succession and giving nobody a chance to answer a single one. Annalise said nothing to anyone after thanking the person who'd lent her their phone.

She didn't need to. Her determination to get them up the hill, into the van and to Montague was so powerful it belied words. As soon as the van slowed in front of them, she loaded her daughter, the dog, the basket and him in quickly.

He held his breath when she sat beside him instead of with Evie, but she didn't pepper him with questions on the ride along the shore toward Montague. The little girl prattled about the singing sands and how they made music and how she could make music on her harmonica and how special the whole place was.

Juan tuned her out, glad he didn't have to reply. He didn't want to talk. He wanted to look out the windows and see if he could replicate when light and shadows had appeared like early morning fog clearing from the river to reveal the far shore.

After almost five weeks of nothingness, would his vision grow stronger? He wished it could be that easy, but he wasn't naive. As they'd hurried up the hill, the shadows closed in around him once more.

Where was the gazebo he'd seen outlined against the sky while he stood on the beach? It had been swallowed by a curtain of gray. Had he strained his eyes by trying to squint up the cliffs and across the sea? How ironic would it be that he'd ruined what might have been his last chance to see?

"Don't be so pessimistic," he muttered.

"You okays?" asked Evie, reaching over the seat to tap her cane against his. "Wants candy?"

"No, thank you. I'm not hungry." His stomach roiled as if he swallowed a cauldron of bubbling soup.

He was relieved when Annalise told Evie to put her seat belt back on. Max's voice was grim as he said he'd get them to Montague as fast as he legally could.

The driver was as *gut* as his word, and the traffic must have cooperated because the van pulled out to pass only two other vehicles during the trip. When they took the roundabout that led into Montague, the van slowed as it encountered more cars and trucks.

Then the van stopped, and Max was climbing out to open the passenger doors. "I'll wait here with the dog. I'll be praying that everything goes well."

Juan clasped the man's arm in thanks before putting his hand on Annalise's arm and letting her lead him into the clinic. For once, he didn't have a chance to sit on the hard chairs. They were immediately escorted into an examination room. The nurse checked his blood pressure and asked a few questions which he stumbled over answering.

His mind was reeling too much to settle on specific details. The words, *I could see something! I could see something!* resonated through his head.

The door opened, and the *doktor* entered. Greeting them, Dr. Armstrong said in his jovial tone, "I didn't expect to have you back so soon. Another cut? From the sand on your shoes, I'd have to say you must have been on the beach. Did you cut yourself on a sawfish?"

Not even Evie giggled.

"I could see things," Juan said. "At the beach."

The *doktor*'s voice changed. At once, he was all business. "What things are you seeing?"

"We went to Basin Head." His voice was unsteady, but he didn't try to fight the tremors of mixed excitement and anxiety. He'd been able to see things, then nothing. Would his sight return? "I was able to tell where the cliffs and sea met."

The *doktor*'s footsteps announced he was going to his supply cupboard. He opened the door, then closed it.

"I'll be looking in your eyes with the ophthalmoscope. You may see a pinprick of light."

Juan strained as Dr. Armstrong held first Juan's left

eye open and then his right, but he didn't see any hint of light. Or was one of the floating sparks created by the ophthalmoscope?

"Can you see anything?" the *doktor* asked.

"No... *Ja*... I don't know."

"You said you were on the beach when you could see the line between the sea and the cliffs?"

"Ja."

Annalise added, "The sun was bright. Very bright. Even with my sunglasses, I had to squint." Her voice softened. "It's cloudy outside now."

"Let's try something." Dr. Armstrong shifted, the breeze left by his motion brushing Juan's face. There was a click. "I turned a light on. To your left."

Juan looked in that direction, trying to pick out a new sparkle among the ones dancing in front of him.

"Don't strain so hard," the *doktor* said. "Your eyes need to adjust to the light."

"Why when I can't see?"

"Because your eyes have really never stopped working. They just haven't been sharing with your brain." Putting a hand on Juan's right shoulder, he said, "Close your eyes, then open them and look to your right." He gave Juan time to follow the order before asking, "Can you see me?"

He blinked once, then a second time before whispering, "I can see what looks like a human-size shadow."

He heard Annalise suck in a deep gasp.

"Can you touch it?" asked the *doktor*.

"I think...so."

He held his breath as he stretched out his hand toward the shadow. If he reached too far, he could fall off the examination table.

Then his fingers poked Dr. Armstrong's chest.

"How about now?" asked the *doktor*. "Don't use your ears to find me. Use your eyes."

Juan closed his eyes, then opened them. The shadow hadn't vanished into the mist. It was still there. His fingers reached out and unerringly touched the *doktor*'s chest.

"I can see!" he choked out.

Annalise had started praying at Basin Head Provincial Park and hadn't stopped through the examination or while they walked back to the van afterward. As she sat between Juan and Evie, she'd thought he would chatter like her daughter. Instead, he was so silent she could discern each raindrop on the van's roof.

When Dr. Armstrong had asked Juan to touch him, she'd leaned forward in her seat, praying he'd still be able to see. Not only would that have been a blessing, but it would mean she didn't have to spend time with a reluctant student.

Who was also an intriguing, handsome man.

When Evie shifted beside her, Annalise couldn't help wondering what the little girl was thinking. Was her daughter wondering if there would come a day when a *doktor* would tell her to keep her eyes closed so light wouldn't hurt them?

Annalise had tried to talk to Evie about if she wished she could view the world as others did. Each time, her daughter had acted as if the question was absurd. Maybe it was, but Annalise wanted to be certain the little girl was happy Wouldn't it be normal for the *kind* to envy others' abilities to do what she had struggled to master?

As if she'd spoken aloud, Evie whispered, "We ares okays just as we ares, *Mamm*, ain't so?"

"*Ja*, we're okay just as we are." She put her arm

around her daughter and snuggled her close. Tears rose in her eyes as she leaned her head against her daughter's.

"Juan is okays, too."

"I am," he said as he tapped his cane on Evie's.

When the little girl giggled and returned the motion, Annalise realized it'd become a secret signal between them. A connection she hadn't noticed before. Juan had become entwined in their lives in ways she couldn't have imagined. What would happen now?

She didn't ask that question then or after Max had dropped them at her farm. When Evie ran inside with Susie on her heels to tell her great-*grossmammi* about the beach and the singing sands, Annalise didn't ask that question. It was pointless when nobody but God knew the answer.

"Do you want to join us for supper?" she asked as she and Juan hurried onto the porch and out of the rain.

"I need time to get my head around what's happening."

"I understand. Let me get a couple of umbrellas, and I'll walk you to your place."

"Annalise."

She turned to face him. His hand beneath her *kapp* cradled her nape as he drew her closer. She should turn away and remind him he'd been her late husband's best friend. She should have, but she didn't. Instead she let her eyes drift closed as his lips brushed hers. His other arm slid around her with a certainty that revealed he could still see shadows.

Had he imagined this as often as she had? Impossible. He'd made it clear in so many ways that he didn't like her.

She hadn't liked him either.

Yet as he captured her lips and deepened the kiss

until her arms were around him, she knew that whether she liked him or not was no longer of importance. She loved him.

The thought pierced her, tearing her from the luscious warmth of his kiss. She stepped away, opened the door and left him standing on the porch, his arms outstretched to hold her.

Dear God, she prayed, *don't let me make another mistake as I did with Boaz.*

Chapter Fourteen

Juan heard his name called as he stepped out on his porch the next day. Hearing the feminine voice, he'd hoped Annalise had come over.

But she hadn't.

"Daisy?" He squinted through the sunshine.

Not much had changed with his eyes since the marvelous afternoon at the beach. He was no longer completely blind, but he couldn't make out the features of someone standing an arm's length from him. More important, he couldn't take care of his farm.

"Ja!" Her cheerful voice rang through the warm morning air. "Get down here and listen to what I've got to tell you."

Regret reminded him that he'd forgotten to talk to Lucas about having a ramp built so his cousin could push her wheelchair up to his porch. He should have been thinking about it and making a plan. Too much else had happened. His eyesight changing and…kissing Annalise.

It would be simple to blame that kiss on his exultance with being able to see shapes and shadows. He could have, but he'd wanted to kiss her for a long time, maybe longer than he'd been blind. She was a fiery, strong-willed woman, and he never could guess how she'd react.

Except when someone needed her help. She didn't hesitate. Her heart was huge, and she led with it.

But she'd fled from him and hadn't come to the farm today as she had every other day.

He tried to push those thoughts aside and concentrate on what had brought his cousin to the farm in the middle of the day.

"What are you doing here, Daisy?" Juan asked. "Is Mattie with you?"

"I'm here to see you. You want to talk with Remy Goyette, ain't so?"

He gawped. Remy Goyette was the captain of the lobster boat Boaz had sailed on the day he died. "I do, but Lucas asked around, and he was told Remy had moved away. Nobody had a new address or phone number for him."

"He came to the farm shop a half hour ago."

"Are you sure?"

Her breath puffed out in a vexed tone. "I'm always sure, Juan! Mattie said she'd keep him there, but she can't do that forever. *Komm mol!* Let's go."

"We'll go by way of Annalise's farm. She may want to meet with him, too."

"I stopped there already. Here she comes."

Juan's breath stopped as he heard hoofbeats along the lane. So much needed to be said between him and Annalise, but it wasn't the right moment.

It took less time than he'd expected to get Daisy's wheelchair into Annalise's wagon. They perched on the seat as the wagon rolled at its top speed along the road. Daisy talked the whole way about how she and

Boppi Lynn had recognized the lobsterman and alerted her sister.

Juan wanted to talk to Annalise. The words seared his tongue, but he couldn't when his cousin kept talking. Wishing he could see Annalise's expression, he had to be patient.

That patience was rewarded when Annalise pulled the wagon into the farm shop's parking lot and Daisy said, "There he is! Right by the side door."

Unable to pick out the man from the shape of the Quonset hut, Juan helped Daisy down and into her chair with a lot of direction from his cousin. She rolled away, running over the side of his right boot. The wheel just missed his toes.

"This way," Annalise said in a whisper as she grasped his hand and slapped it onto her arm.

His cane couldn't keep up with her pace, so he didn't try. He trusted she wouldn't steer him into something.

The lobsterman greeted them in a booming voice. When Mattie suggested they speak in her office, Juan sensed Annalise's relief through her taut arm. They went with Remy into the small space, which held a table and several chairs in front of a pair of filing cabinets.

Mattie brought in *kaffi* and shooed her younger sister out before saying, "If you need anything, give a yell." She closed the door before Juan could thank her.

"Remy," Juan said as he wove his fingers around his cup, "I don't know if you've met Annalise Overgard."

"Overgard? Like Boaz?" the lobsterman asked.

"*Ja*. He was my husband." Her voice was little more than a wisp of sound.

When Remy's weathered face turned gray, Annalise prayed Remy wouldn't race out of the office. She could see he was thinking of doing that.

Then he reached for the sugar and spooned enough in to make his *kaffi* sickly sweet. He cleared this throat. "I'm sorry for his passing, Mrs. Overgard."

"*Danki*, and Annalise will do."

"Yeah. I remember. Boaz once said you plain folks don't take to titles."

"So you and Boaz were friends?" She was grateful when Juan took her hand beneath the table as she dared to ask the questions that had plagued her during the grief-filled months since Boaz's death.

"Friends? I wouldn't say that. Boaz pestered me until I agreed to take him out." Remy ran his hand through his hair, then put his battered cap on his head. Taking a deep sip of *kaffi*, he said, "To be honest, I got tired of him hanging around, so I told him he could come. As long as he stayed out of the way while we worked."

"How many were on the boat that day?" Juan asked.

"Counting Boaz, there were four of us. Was going to make for tight quarters when a bunch of the traps were on deck, but we're used to it."

Annalise asked, "Was Boaz on the deck, too?"

"Not all the time. When we were checking the traps and bringing them onboard because it was our last time out for the season, I had him stay in the shelter and watch the helm. It wasn't necessary because we learned a long time ago how to keep the boat steady while hauling in the traps, but he seemed to think it was an important job." He arched a brow. "I didn't disabuse him of that notion because it kept him from being underfoot."

"If he was safe at the helm…"

Remy's face dropped along with his voice. "He didn't stay there as he told me he would. Sometime when we were about twenty kilometers out from Montague, he must have come aft. By that time, the whole stern was stacked with traps and bins for the lobsters. He must have gone behind them. Not that he needed to sneak around. We never would have seen him because we were busy. The waves were getting really high, so we were hurrying to get our traps out. The boat began to rock hard. At one point, I told Boaz to lash himself to the helm. I didn't have time to check if he'd obeyed. I was thinking only about getting our traps and us back to shore before the worst of the storm hit. When we realized he wasn't aboard, we backtracked, looking for him. We searched for more than an hour, but couldn't stay out any longer or we would have been swamped and lost. It was the eye of a hurricane going east of the Island. Remember?"

"I remember," she said. Did he expect she'd forget anything about the day of her husband's death?

Abruptly, as his face became another shade paler, she realized poor Remy was more uncomfortable than she was while he related what he knew of Boaz's last hours. Why hadn't she seen right from the beginning that he carried a burden of guilt as heavy as his boat?

Stretching across the table, she put her hand on his clenched fist. "*Danki*, Remy, for sharing what happened that day."

He met her eyes for the first time, and she saw thankfulness in them. "Anything else?"

"I don't think so," she said to halt Juan from speaking. "I really appreciate you taking this time to talk with us."

"My pleasure," he replied, though she knew it'd been anything but pleasant for him to relive those hours. He stood and left the room.

Juan gasped. "You must have had more questions. I do."

"What does it matter? Why make the man suffer by going through everything? It won't change what happened."

"That was our last chance to find out the truth."

"The truth is Boaz didn't heed the captain's orders, and he was swept overboard. That cost him his life."

"I wanted to know what happened."

"You do know," she argued, her temper rising. "You know everything Remy does."

He leaned his faced against his clenched fists. "It's not enough. I need to know if it would have been the same if I had been there. Would everything have ended differently if…?"

When his voice trailed off, she comprehended what he hadn't said. She put her hand on his shoulder. "You feel guilty about Boaz's death?"

"Ja."

"Why?"

He looked so intently at her that she wondered how much better he could see. "Boaz asked me to go with him that day. I needed to get the animals ready for the incoming storm. I asked him to wait until another day when we could both go."

"Which he didn't want to do." She sighed. "Boaz was so desperate to learn how to pilot a boat and make a living on the sea, he wouldn't listen to reason. I pleaded with him to wait until spring when the waters would be calm, and he could see how things were at the beginning of the lobster season. I mentioned spring would be a *gut* time to find a part-time job to try the work."

"You did?"

"He was my husband. I wanted him to be happy, but I reminded him that it was going to be the crew's last trip until spring."

"He didn't listen to you either." Sorrow deepened his voice.

"No. He was so gung ho to get out on the water. He must have known, as I did, that a single voyage wouldn't have given him an inkling of the work he needed to learn. He was pushing to sell the farm, so we could move to Montague and buy a used boat. It didn't make any sense to do that in December."

"He wanted to fix up a boat. He talked about that a lot."

"Not to me. He said with prices going up, we must take advantage of the deal he'd chanced upon."

Juan sighed. "It sounds as if he wasn't honest with either of us."

"Or about either of us."

He nodded. "I've come to realize that, too. Where do we go from here?"

With her emotions too raw from everything that had happened in the past twenty-four hours, she pretended not to understand what he meant. She pushed a cheery tone into her answer. "I don't know about you, but I need to get home and finish up my chores."

He opened his mouth to reply, then closed it and got to his feet. As he grasped his cane before going to the door, she ached to call him back. Instead she let him go, and the wall they'd torn down together rose between them again. She wasn't sure if this time, it could come down.

"Something's wrong with you, Annalise." *Grossmammi* Fern rinsed the pan Annalise had used for making hamburgers for their midday meal and set it on the drainer. "What is it?"

Annalise considered saying she was unnerved by

what the lobsterman had told her at the farm shop a couple of hours ago. Yet, her uneasiness was less about Remy and more about Juan.

"I've been thinking," she said, "about something you told me the day Juan ate with us after his tests in Charlottetown."

"So long ago?" The older woman laughed. "You want to talk to me about it? You do know I sometimes forget what I had for dinner by the time we get to supper." Something in Annalise's expression must have tipped her off because she said, "I can see this is serious. What did I say that night that's upset you?"

"You saw me look at the table while we were serving the meal. You looked, too. When you saw Juan and Evie sitting together on the bench, you said Evie thought of Juan differently than she had Boaz. That Juan was her friend, not her *daed*."

"I don't understand why that would upset you."

"It didn't." She faltered, not sure why she'd brought up the subject. Plowing ahead, she said, "It was what you said next."

"Which was?"

"That Evie knew the difference between her *daed* and Boaz, and I should, too." She lowered her eyes. "I'm sorry if you thought I was leaving my mourning behind too soon."

The older woman cupped Annalise's chin in her hand. Tilting Annalise's head up so their eyes were even, *Grossmammi* Fern said, "Boaz Overgard was my grandson, and I loved him in spite of his faults. In spite of them! I saw each and every one of them, how he was selfish and how he became bored with each thing he believed would make him happy." Her mouth tightened into a straight line. "I also saw how weak he was when his daughter was born and how he put all the responsibility on you, which you shouldered without complaint."

More tears pricked her eyes, and she blinked hard. "I complained. I'm ashamed that I did."

"Why? You carry a heavy load. To say you're tired is not a complaint. It's a fact. Not once have I heard you say that you regret having Evie in your life."

"Because I don't!"

"My grandson did."

She gasped as *Grossmammi* Fern corroborated what Annalise had secretly suspected. The very thing that she hadn't wanted to believe: Boaz hadn't wanted to have a blind *kind* as his.

Grossmammi Fern clasped her hands around Annalise's. "*Liebling*, I know he loved you. How could he not? He was too busy looking for an escape from his responsibilities. He saw in you someone strong enough to pick up the pieces when he went on to the next thing he thought would give him the excitement he craved." Her voice gentled. "What I meant when I said you should remember Boaz and Juan are two different men is that you shouldn't let your experiences with my grandson taint what you and Juan could share."

Heat rose up Annalise's face. Her attraction to Juan had been so new and uncertain that night; yet, *Grossmammi* Fern had sensed the truth Annalise hadn't been ready to face then.

Or now. As she began to dry the dishes, she changed the subject to the dogs, a topic *Grossmammi* Fern always enjoyed. When she saw the older woman's twinkling eyes, Annalise knew she wasn't fooling *Grossmammi* Fern.

As soon as they were finished with the dishes, Annalise went to her workshop to try to sort out her thoughts. She stayed there for over an hour, but made a mess of everything she touched because her mind wouldn't stay on her task. Instead, she found herself dripping paint on the dala horses, her apron and the floor as she stared out the window toward Juan's farm.

Annalise gave up before she ruined everything she'd worked on. Returning to the house, she discovered *Grossmammi* Fern sewing in the living room. Mei-Mei was curled up at her feet. Odd… Susie had been coming in each afternoon to spend time with the smaller dog. Annalise hadn't seen her on the porch either.

"Is Evie upstairs?" Annalise asked.

Grossmammi Fern put her sewing on her lap. "I thought she was with you."

"No. She must be upstairs."

"I haven't heard a sound, and you know how the floors creak."

Annalise didn't wait to hear any more. She hurried up the stairs and along the hall to her daughter's room.

The door was open, but the room was empty. Evie's cane was gone along with her bonnet. On the bed was an open book. It was the only one in braille that Boaz had ever given his daughter. Not surprisingly it was the tale of a lobsterman. The picture showed a boat pulled up on bright red sands.

Evie had been in the other room when Daisy came with the news that she'd seen Remy. If Evie had heard…

Racing down the stairs, Annalise tried not to think of the number of cars and trucks her daughter might encounter on her way to the farm shop. She called to *Grossmammi* Fern to let her know that Annalise would be back as soon as she found Evie.

Please, God, let me find her safe.

* * *

With a shake of his head, Juan tossed the broken metal onto the pieces that once had been his antique tractor. He'd come out to the shed, hoping he'd find answers. His eyesight had been a little clearer as the day went on, and he'd managed to feed his animals. He hoped within a few weeks to be able to handle the milking as well. He had so many people to repay for their help.

If his eyes continued to improve, he might be able to work in the fields. He had a couple of months before he'd need to harvest his potatoes and corn. Before the accident, he and Lucas had discussed planting Irish cobbler potatoes. He was glad they hadn't. Those early potatoes would have been ready next month.

"Juan? Are you here?" came a frantic shout.

He pushed his way out of the shed. He caught sight of a form running toward him. "Annalise? What is it?"

"Have you seen Evie?"

"No. Is she missing?" He didn't give her a chance to answer. "That's a stupid question. Of course, she's missing if you're looking for her. How long has she been gone?"

"At the most an hour or two. I saw her at dinner, then she went upstairs for her afternoon nap. Usually Evie finds me when she wakes up because we have a cookie and *millich* as a treat for her being *gut* during quiet time." Her voice deepened with anguish. "I was in my shop and time got away from me."

"She could get quite a ways in an hour or two."

"I know."

"Susie is so smart. Do you think she could find—?"

"Susie is missing, too."

"Mei-Mei?"

"She's fine. Did Evie and Susie come here?"

He shook his head. "If they did, I never heard them, and I would have. The goats start making noise as soon as they realize Evie or Susie is nearby."

Annalise groaned. "Then it's as I feared. She's gone to the farm shop. We've got to get to her before she steps out in front of a car."

"Susie is with her."

"She's a *gut* dog, but she's not trained to guide Evie. *Komm mol!* We've got to find them before they're hurt or…"

She didn't finish. She didn't have to. Juan heard *or killed* in his mind.

Chapter Fifteen

The Celtic Knoll Farm Shop was busy when Annalise drove her wagon into the parking lot for the second time that day. The silver Quonset hut glistened in the late-afternoon sunshine. Buggies and cars filled the available parking slots, and customers created a steady stream in and out of the wide door at the side. Fresh vegetables and the province's famous potatoes were stacked in bins just inside the shop.

Annalise ran to the side door. She scanned the interior, spotting Mattie at the cash register.

"Wait here, Juan," she said.

She didn't pause for his answer. She rushed to the cash register.

Juan's cousin gave her a warm smile. "What can I do for you, Annalise? Oh, there's Juan! I didn't think you'd be back again so soon. Can I help you?"

"*Ja.* Have you seen Evie?" she asked.

Mattie's smile wavered, then vanished. "No. What's going on?"

"She was supposed to be taking a nap, but it looks as if she slipped out of the house after she went up to her room a couple of hours ago." Repeating the facts made her heart ache more.

Gentle fingers brushed her arm, and she looked over her shoulder at Juan. Though she knew he couldn't see her face, his gaze met hers with a precision that amazed her. She was accustomed to Evie knowing how to connect with her, but it was a treasured gift each time he did the same.

"What makes you think she came here?" Mattie asked.

Juan explained how Evie had overheard Daisy talking about the lobsterman earlier. "Annalise thinks she may have come here to find out what else Daisy knows. We've looked for her on the way here, and Lucas and a couple of others are checking the fields in case she decided to go through one of them."

"She wouldn't," Annalise was certain of that. The rows of potato hills were almost impossible for her daughter to navigate. "Mattie, will you check with Daisy to see if she's talked to Evie?"

Mattie came around the counter, calling to her cousin Daryn to take over. As the lanky teen greeted the next customer, she said, "Daisy's been putting groceries on the shelves, but if she's not here, she's probably in the back."

Daisy wasn't among the shelves, so Mattie disappeared past a swinging door. Wringing her hands, Annalise rocked from one foot to the other as she heard Mattie call her sister's name.

If Evie wasn't here, then where could she be?

"God's watching over her," Juan said from behind her. "You know that."

"I do," she said, not moving her gaze from the swinging door. "I didn't think you did."

"Because I was angry at God for letting me lose my

sight doesn't mean I stopped believing He's watching over us."

The door opened. Mattie came out, her face ashen. "Daisy's gone."

"Any idea where?" Juan asked.

"No."

"Wouldn't she leave you a note?" Annalise asked.

"She would, or..." She glanced toward the teenager working at the register. "Or she'd tell someone."

Mattie sprinted across the store, edging around her customers to return to the till. Annalise hooked her arm through Juan's and led him after his cousin.

"Daryn, have you seen Daisy?" Mattie asked.

The teenager's smile fell off his face, replaced by a sudden flash of guilt.

"*Ja*," he said, but added nothing more.

"Where did you see her last? When?"

He looked chagrined. "When I helped her and your little girl, Annalise, into a car. That big dog got in, too."

"Whose car?"

"I don't know, but Daisy knew the woman."

Juan's annoyance exploded out. "Did you stop to think it might not have been a *gut* idea to send them off in a car?"

"Daisy knew the woman. Daisy makes *gut* decisions." Daryn turned to Mattie. "You said so just the other day."

"*Ja*, but I was talking about arranging groceries on the shelves, not heading off who knows where with a little girl and a huge dog."

"Did you know the driver?" Annalise asked, trying to keep the conversation from being derailed.

"I think so," Daryn said. "Her name is Joni something or other."

"Livingstone?" Mattie asked.

He nodded. "I think so. She buys lots of homemade root beer."

Mattie turned to Annalise and grabbed her arm. Steering her and Juan away from the register, she smiled at her customers before lowering her voice, "I know Joni Livingstone pretty well. She's a nice lady. She lives out near Souris, but drives here to get vegetables as well as root beer."

"Souris?" gasped Annalise. "That's near—"

Juan interrupted, "Basin Head Provincial Park. Evie loved the beach. Maybe she couldn't wait to go back."

"We need to get there right away. If we can get Max—"

"I'll make the call." Mattie ran toward her office.

Annalise's knees threatened to betray her as she went outside. When Juan took her hand, she was grateful for his strength. How right *Grossmammi* Fern had been! Juan Kuepfer was different from Boaz Overgard because he was there when she needed him.

As soon as the white van pulled into the parking lot, Max jumped out and opened the door. "If you'll get in, we'll find your little girl, Annalise."

"Danki." She slid into the back seat. As Juan sat beside her, after telling Mattie he'd let her know as soon as they had any information, she tried to relax against the seat. It was impossible when she was as tense as an electric line in a windstorm.

The van sped toward the provincial park. Max paid no attention to the speed limit, though he slowed for stop signs before gunning the engine to rush toward the park again. The parking lot overlooking the beach was empty.

As they got out of the car, Max asked, "Do you think the girls are in one of the buildings? I can search them."

"Go ahead," Annalise said. "When Evie gets an idea in her head, she's like Boaz. Nothing knocks it out."

"I get that. How are you doing?" Juan asked as they walked to the gate at the top of the hill.

"I keep telling myself she's got Daisy, Susie and God watching over her."

"I hope that's enough."

"Me, too." She took a single step, then Juan's hand settled on her arm.

"Wait," he said. "There!"

"Where?"

"Farther down. I hear something. Listen." He put his finger to her lips. Did he feel the same connection she did to him since their kiss? No, she wouldn't think of that. She had to focus on finding Evie.

At first, she heard only the crash of the waves. *Try harder.* She heard her heartbeat, then she heard... Was that music? From someone's phone or a radio?

No!

It was a harmonica being played with more enthusiasm than skill.

"Evie!" she cried at the same time Juan asked, "Where is she?"

"I see someone!" He tugged on her arm. "Down at the bottom of the hill. Is it Evie?"

"No, it's Daisy." In front of the outdoor shower where the path curved toward the storage buildings, Daisy sat in her wheelchair, her face turned toward the water. If Evie had gone in...

No! She wasn't going to think about the worst. She was going to trust God to bring about the best ending possible.

"Go! Don't wait for me," he ordered.

"The hill is steep, and—"

He grasped her shoulders and turned her to face him.

His expression was grim. "I'll make it down the hill or I won't. You can't worry about that. You need to find Evie."

She knew he was right. Racing down the hill, she almost tripped on loose stones.

"Hey!" Daisy called, waving. "Why are you here?"

"Why are *you* here?" Annalise waved aside her own question. "Where's Evie?"

"On the beach." She patted the arm of her wheelchair. "I didn't go with her because I could have gotten stuck in the sand, and Boppi Lynn gets scared we'll wash away."

"Will you be all right here?" Annalise asked.

"Been so far."

She couldn't argue with the teenager's logic. "Okay. Stay here while I get Evie and the dog."

"I'm coming with you," Juan said as he caught up with them.

She relented. Peering through the buildings, she saw the tide was low. The sandbar was a miniature island. Nobody stood on it.

Juan said, "She's on the beach below the cliffs."

Before she could ask him how he could be so certain, she heard the faint music followed by a dog's deep bark. He must have picked up the notes before she did.

"Go, go," Juan urged. "I'll get there when I can."

She didn't ask him if he was sure. She ran along the boardwalk. Coming out between the two beach sheds, she followed the boardwalk to its end in the rusty sand.

There, on the sand, her daughter danced with Susie. The dog carried Evie's cane in her mouth. When had Evie taught the dog that trick? Her daughter was playing the harmonica, but the sound of the waves drowned out the melody.

"Evie!" Annalise shouted.

The little girl whirled, and a broad grin stretched her round cheeks. "Sees? Me no goes into the river to rides out into the ocean. Me stays on the sand until I goes to school. First school, then riding the run, ain't so?"

"Ja." She knelt on the sand and enveloped her daughter in an embrace. "Evie, why did you go away without telling me?"

"I tells you. My book tells you."

"The story of the lobsterman and his boat?"

"Daed gaves it to me. I comes here to make the sand sings for *Daed.* Listens!" She put the harmonica to her mouth and began to play what was, Annalise realized, a slightly off-key rendition of the lullaby Boaz had sung to her each night before he stopped tucking her in. "It's *Daed*'s special song."

"You remember that?"

"I dos now. I forgets about it till you sings it to me, *Mamm.* I remembers." Tears welled up in her eyes. "How coulds I forgets about it? It was *Daed*'s song."

"Which he shared with his beloved daughter," Juan said as he put his hand on Annalise's shoulder.

"Cans he hear it, Juan?"

"Of course, he can because he was your *daed.*"

Annalise looked at him. Nothing on his face suggested he wasn't being honest, but she'd never heard Boaz speak lovingly of their daughter. She couldn't ask, not when Evie was right there, but her heart needed to know the truth.

Later, she promised.

Juan kept his arm around Annalise's shoulders, not surprised they were trembling.

"Ready to go, Jolly-Jelly-Evie-Belly?" Annalise asked, holding out her hand to Evie.

The little girl didn't move. Instead she asked, "Juan, ares you sure that if I plays loud enough, *Daed* hears, ain't so?"

"I'm sure your *daed* loves every note." He was moved by her faith that hadn't been shaken as his had. Standing on the beach, he could discern a variety of dark and lighter shapes. He could see Susie's silhouette as the dog chased the waves, trying to herd them in the direction she wanted them to go.

Looking up toward the hill, he squinted. Was that wavy shape Daisy in her wheelchair? Annalise had told him to have faith by not fighting the timeline God had set for his recovery. She'd been right. What he wanted was irrelevant. God was in charge, and Juan would be smart not to forget that.

As Evie called to the dog and ran toward where Daisy waited, he fell into step beside Annalise.

"You're weeping," she said as they reached the boardwalk.

He touched his cheek. "I am."

"Why?"

"I know you want me to say it's because I'm so happy we've found Evie, Daisy and Susie safe and sound. It is, but…" He struggled for the words to explain what was going on in his heart.

Maybe he shouldn't say anything. Annalise was reunited with her daughter, and there should have been happiness ricocheting through him.

"Evie will never know the joy," he said, "of having light come into her life as I do."

"Never say never, someone once told me," she said with a chuckle.

He gave a feigned groan. "Eating one's words makes for a disgusting meal."

"I may be doing the same because I thought Boaz had no use for Evie."

"We'll never know what drove him to do the things he did, but I do know he loved Evie. He didn't speak of her often. When he did, I could tell he loved her."

"Or he wanted to."

"You might be right because he couldn't hide that he didn't know how to deal with a blind *kind*." He paused and brought her to face him. "But I'm sure of one thing, Annalise. He loved you."

"I'm not so sure he ever did."

"Don't you see? You were his dream come true."

"Until he got another dream and another and another." She sighed. "But that was the way God made him, and nothing could change that. I guess Boaz did love me...in his own way."

"As I love you in my own way."

She choked on the retort she'd been about to make. "You love me?"

"*Ja*. I know you might not be able to say the same."

As if they were alone on the beach instead of with Evie, Daisy, Susie and Max, she stood on tiptoe and pressed her mouth to his. He held her close, exploring every curve of her lips. He needed to ask her to be his wife. That could wait while he savored this kiss he prayed would be repeated often for the rest of their lives together.

Epilogue

"What do you think?"

Annalise pretended to pause to consider the project Juan and his brother had been working on since breakfast. "Are you sure it's the right angle?"

"Very sure," Juan said with a laugh. "Lucas made me measure the support boards at least a million times."

"Don't exaggerate." Lucas clapped him on the back. "It was only half a million times."

"It's a nice ramp," she said. "Daisy's going to appreciate your hard work."

As Lucas gathered a handful of tools and carried them to the shed where the tractor once had been stored, Annalise helped Juan collect the others. He hadn't completely recovered his vision, and glasses helped him compensate. He joked they were as thick and heavy as a soda bottle, but they were the first thing he reached for each morning.

She smiled. She was certain of that fact because she'd been by his side each morning since their wedding in July. Two months of marriage had proved she'd been right to give him an enthusiastic *Ja* to his proposal, though Evie had been more effusive, dancing and singing and playing raucous songs on her harmonica when she heard the news.

They were living most of the time at Annalise's house, but they planned to move into Juan's over the winter. Work had already been started on building two extra rooms on the house. One for *Grossmammi* Fern and the other for the future.

They'd spoken to the bishop about selling Annalise's farm, but nothing would be done until after the harvest. Also a new shed needed to be constructed to hold Annalise's woodworking equipment. Juan was eager to learn more about using them as his vision had improved.

That wasn't for today...

"A *gut* project well done," Annalise said as she handed her husband the toolbox.

"Though it took long enough." He ran his hand along the rail. "I've come to realize that putting things off until tomorrow isn't the best way to live my life. I promised I'd have a ramp for Daisy to come into the house before I moved in. It's taken six months to do as I said. I won't make that mistake again."

"Evie is going to love it." She laughed. "Along with Susie and Mei-Mei. They're going to chase each other up, down and under it. Well, maybe Mei-Mei beneath it. Susie won't fit. Evie won't either. She's growing so fast."

He took her hand. "Who knows what Evie will be able to do if she gets into that new research study?"

"Let's see if the specialist agrees to include her first."

"You don't fool me. You're as excited about it as I am."

"I am." She laughed as he put his toolbox on the porch. "What a blessing having Evie see anything would be!"

"I knew you were excited." He chuckled.

Sitting beside him on the edge of the deck, she rested

her head on his shoulder. She had something else to be eager about, but she needed to wait a few more weeks before sharing her suspicions that by this time next year, they'd have another member in their family.

A shout came from the lane, and Annalise saw Juan's cousins—and hers now—as well as their families coming toward the house. Everyone wanted to see what Juan and Lucas had been building.

"Shall we go and greet them?" he asked, holding out his hand as he stood.

"As long as I'm with you."

"Always." He kissed her lightly, but with a sparkle in his eyes that told her he planned on many more kisses once they were alone.

She couldn't wait.

* * * * *

*If you enjoyed this story, don't miss these
other books from Jo Ann Brown:*

The Amish Suitor
The Amish Christmas Cowboy
The Amish Bachelor's Baby
The Amish Widower's Twins
An Amish Christmas Promise
An Amish Easter Wish
An Amish Mother's Secret Past
An Amish Holiday Family
Building Her Amish Dream
Snowbound Amish Christmas

Find more great reads at www.LoveInspired.com

Dear Reader,

Welcome back to Prince Edward Island…and the warm weather! After a tough winter, spring always blooms with glorious flowers and sunshine and new crops in the fields. It's the season for new beginnings. Annalise Overgard and Juan Kuepfer must face challenges they couldn't have imagined the year before. They have to be brave enough—or have faith enough—to trust that God is with them even when they feel most alone. I know my own life would be simpler if I could just remember that simple truth each time I'm confronted by the unexpected.

Visit me at www.joannbrownbooks.com. And look for my next book set on Prince Edward Island coming soon!

Wishing you many blessings,
Jo Ann Brown

COMING NEXT MONTH FROM
Love Inspired

THE TEACHER'S CHRISTMAS SECRET
Seven Amish Sisters • by Emma Miller

Cora Koffman dreams of being a teacher. But the job is given to newcomer Tobit Lapp instead. When an injury forces the handsome widower to seek out Cora's help, can they get along for the sake of the students? Or will his secret ruin the holidays?

TRUSTING HER AMISH RIVAL
Bird-in-Hand Brides • by Jackie Stef

Shy Leah Fisher runs her own bakery shop in town. When an opportunity to expand her business comes from childhood bully Silas Riehl, she reluctantly agrees to the partnership. They try to keep things professional, but will their past get in the way?

A COMPANION FOR CHRISTMAS
K-9 Companions • by Lee Tobin McClain

When her Christmas wedding gets canceled, first-grade teacher Kelly Walsh takes a house-sitting gig with her therapy dog on the outskirts of town for a much-needed break. Then her late sister's ex-boyfriend, Alec Wilkins, unexpectedly arrives with his toddler daughter, and this holiday refuge could become something more...

REDEEMING THE COWBOY
Stone River Ranch • by Lisa Jordan

After his rodeo career is ruined, cowboy Barrett Stone did not expect to be working with Piper Healy, his late best friend's wife, on his family's ranch. She blames him for her husband's death. Can he prove he's more than the reckless cowboy she used to know?

FINDING THEIR CHRISTMAS HOME
by Donna Gartshore

Returning home after years abroad, Jenny Powell is eager to spend the holidays with her grandmother at their family home. Then she discovers that old flame David Hart is staying there with his twin girls as well. Could it be the second chance that neither of them knew they needed?

THEIR SURPRISE SECOND CHANCE
by Lindi Peterson

Widower Adam Hawk is figuring out how to parent his young daughter when an old love, Nicole St. John, returns unexpectedly—with a fully grown child he never knew he had. Nicole needs his help guiding their troubled son. Can they work together for a second chance at family?

LOOK FOR THESE AND OTHER LOVE INSPIRED BOOKS WHEREVER BOOKS ARE SOLD, INCLUDING MOST BOOKSTORES, SUPERMARKETS, DISCOUNT STORES AND DRUGSTORES.

LICNM0823

HARLEQUIN
PLUS

Try the best multimedia subscription service for romance readers like you!

Read, Watch and Play.

Experience the easiest way to get the romance content you crave.

Start your **FREE TRIAL** at
www.harlequinplus.com/freetrial.